This is odd, even for me. I look around the deli, there are no children anywhere. There's no TV reporting a missing child, no radio. No one's even on their phones. Just a couple people eating lovely sandwiches, much like the one that's getting cold in front of me. Yet here I am, with a blazing headache, looking at a woman in her twenties, and wondering if my "gift" just expanded to adults or if my mental wires are completely crossed.

I suppose it could just be a regular old headache.

But we all know it's not.

The pregnant lady comes up to the order window. Now, since Cassie's been out of my sight for a couple minutes I haven't a clue if this person in front of me is the same person I saw three minutes ago.

Isn't my life super fun?

"Cassie? Cassie Wilson?"

"Yes? Oh, Nora! Hi!"

That's where my social skills end. Now what do I say? "I thought it was you. I just wanted to say…hi. So, hi."

"Oh aren't you so nice? Well thanks for stopping in and enjoy your lunch!" Cassie reaches out and touches my shoulder.

And the room goes black.

WARNING
IN
WAUKESHA

A NORA HILL MYSTERY
BY
S. J. BRADLEY

<u>Other books from SJB Books Authors</u>

<u>S. J. Bradley, Inspirational mystery</u>

Missing in Manitowoc, Nora Hill Mystery #1

Superhero in Superior, Nora Hill Mystery #2

<u>Sarah J. Bradley, contemporary romantic suspense</u>

Dream in Color

Love Is… (3 Rock Harbor Short Romances)

Lies in Chance (Rock Harbor Chronicles #1)

Fresh Ice (Rock Harbor Chronicles #2)

A Hero's Spark (Rock Harbor Chronicles #3)

<u>Sarah Jayne Brewster, nonfiction/humor</u>

Not While I'm Chewing: Elsie W's FIRST Book

Unsafe at Any Speed: Elsie W's OTHER Book

WARNING IN WAUKESHA

Cover art by Sarah J. Bradley/ SJB BOOKS

Twitter: @sarah_theauthor

Web: authorsarahjbradley.blogspot.com

Facebook: https:// www.facebook.com/sjbbooks/

Published in the United States of America

The preacher said he was a good man.

His brother said he was a good friend.

The women in the two black veils didn't bother to cry.

Carrie Underwood

FRIDAY 2:00 PM

I'd like to say that I broke my right leg and foot doing something heroic, or maybe something cool and adventurous. I'm told normal people break bones by playing some sport or long distance running or maybe falling from a rock wall at an auto show. I've seen TV shows where firemen broke bones because they rescued someone from a burning building, but then had to leap out of a second story window to save themselves.

Any of that would be so much better than my reality.

Nope, I'm sitting here on this impossibly clean white couch my mom calls a settee. Yes, in my mother's house there are pieces of furniture with names like 'settee.' I'm staring at the beast cast my nieces and nephews have been drawing on for the last four weeks. I'm trapped, living in a makeshift bedroom on the first floor because I can't navigate up the stairs to my own room.

I can't even drive my beloved Forester.

And how did this come to pass? How did I manage to render myself virtually helpless and at the mercy of my mother's overly watchful ministrations?

I kicked one of the stacks of storage boxes in the garage and it fell on me, breaking the fibula in two places and crushing all five long bones in my foot.

Now the next question, of course, is, Nora, why on earth did you kick one of your hoarder mother's mountainous stack of plastic storage boxes filled with all of your dearly departed father's theological books?

9

I'm not even sure anymore, how I managed to call up the kind of rage it took for me to endanger my ability to leave Brenda Hill's sensible two-story sanctuary in Waukesha, Wisconsin.

Oh wait, yes I do.

It all goes back to Jack.

My drive from Superior, Wisconsin back to Waukesha on July Fourth weekend took a little longer than expected because I was in a sort of surprisingly emotional state. I was, I think, broken hearted. I'm not sure, because it's not like I've had a lot of experience in the world of romance and heartbreak. I mean, it could have just been a mild case of hypothermia from swimming in the icy waters of Lake Superior. But I have to attribute my mental confusion and strange tearful moments to the fight I had with Jack Terrell in the parking lot of a little church in Superior.

Jack was my high school crush, but when we reconnected at our high school reunion earlier this summer, I had zero intention of feeling anything for him. I've worked very hard in my life to shut down feelings that might hurt me. Life for me is far too thorny as it is to also involve something as volatile as romantic love into the mix.

I have prosopagnosia, face blindness, a condition that makes it impossible to remember faces or voices for longer than the time it takes to toast a bagel. When you deal with this impairment, you learn to put up walls and protect yourself from inevitable pain. Human connections are dependent on recognition and communication. Thanks to face blindness, I'm terrible at both.

But the fight we had wasn't about face blindness. I'm not even sure how we got to the point where Jack yelled at me in the church parking lot with the parishioners looking on. I can't blame any of them for staring at us. It's not every Sunday a congregation gets to watch as a purple-haired, tattooed woman overflows the bathroom with a single piece of toilet tissue and then gets a full volume lecture on why she's a terrible candidate for a mother figure in a teen girl's life.

Oh yes, my world is full of strange twists and turns.

The toilet tissue thing I chalk up to the fact that it doesn't seem to matter where I go to church, disaster follows me. It's like God's telling me that maybe He doesn't want me in church or something, although my dearly departed father, a minister while he was with us, always told me God wanted all His children to visit His house.

I don't know, maybe I'm looking in the wrong house or something. For my whole life I've felt like everyone's doing this dance and I have no idea what the steps are. My sisters, Lily and Rose, are just the most physically beautiful women, and they are able to go to church and raise kids and pray at every meal and never once has anyone ever yelled at them in a parking lot. My mother is pretty much stiff-postured perfection. My father, I'm convinced, was what they meant when they said people were created in the image of God. Meanwhile, I'm short, I've got that really chic, malnourished look going, no matter how much I eat. Also, I have a nasty habit of coloring my hair or getting a tattoo or piercing something every time I feel like I'm getting to close to normal. I'm like one of those weird bugs on the animal channel that has all kinds of stripes and colors to warn other animals to just stay away.

I'm not sure how Jack and I even got to a place where the words "mother" and "figure" were used in the same sentence as my name but it had something to do with his daughter, Samantha. Sam's a little bit of a precocious outsider in her own age group. She and I clicked the moment we met. Sam calls me a couple times a week and we usually wind up watching a couple episodes of "Quantum Leap" on Netflix.

Or we used to. Since Superior, I haven't heard from either one of them.

I shouldn't feel all that upset, it's not like I was connected to them for a lifetime or anything. The reunion where I caught up with Jack and met Sam was two months ago. Seriously, now that I think about it, Jack's whole "You're a bad influence on my daughter" thing was way over the top given the time frame. It's not like I'm an important part of their lives.

And I sure don't make deep connections with people that quickly. Or ever. Nope.

Oh, sure I miss watching "Quantum Leap" with the kid. But that's it. I'm not emotionally invested. I've spent most of my adult life keeping myself at arm's reach just so I don't get hurt in this very situation. I'm just annoyed because I liked talking to Sam. She's sort of an odd duck, like me, and she's not even related to me.

And okay, if I'm being honest, Jack's a really good guy to talk to. He sort of gets my face blindness and doesn't treat me like a child or a mental patient. Which is nice.

Plus he's got these fantastic blue eyes that stick in my brain when everything else washes away.

12

"Nora, Kevin's here for his driving lesson." My mother's all-too-polite voice breaks into my thoughts.

I'm actually grateful for that. I don't want to think about Jack right now…or his blue eyes.

"Don't keep him waiting out there on the porch."

"Why doesn't he just come in for a minute while I'm getting onto my crutches?"

My mother face pinches, as if she's smelling something sour. "Eleanor, you know I love my grandchildren, every one of them. But Kevin is such a loud boy, and he stomps everywhere with those big shoes of his and…and he got maple syrup on the settee and I haven't been able to get that stain out yet."

That stain got there, if memory serves, about ten years ago. Kevin was six. Mom had the cushion cleaned six different ways. Honestly, if there's still a stain there, she's the only one who can see it.

I'm not going to make a big deal out of it, though, because I finally get to leave the house. See, "driving lesson" is code for "get Nora out of the house for a couple hours."

Kevin, my sister Rose's oldest boy, has been assigned to me as a chauffeur. He just turned sixteen and is eager to drive, but no one in this extended family of ours has time to help the boy. The family had a meeting, which is actually a nice way of saying my mother invited everyone over for dinner so she and my two sisters could discuss how to handle me. At such "meetings" my brothers-in-law and I sat quietly like children awaiting punishment, eating what was put in front of us and not questioning anything. The decision the women folk came to was that my broken bones were actually a gift from God and should be looked upon and used as such.

I am to teach Kevin how to drive and in return he's going to drive me to and from my pressing errands.

So glad my fractures are a cause for thanksgiving.

Here's what it all comes down to: I don't have any pressing errands. I'm perfectly fine sitting on my mother's settee, glaring at her until she answers the questions I asked her when I got home from Superior.

See, I have never felt like I fit in the family. Kevin, in all his gawky, lunky teen-age angst, is the one person I feel kind of connected to. I've always been the dirty daughter, the screw up, the one not good enough. When Dad was alive, it wasn't as bad because he had a way of making me feel okay about not fitting in. But he's been gone since I graduated from high school and the gap between my perfect mother and sisters and me grows bigger every day.

It doesn't help any that during a heated phone conversation my mother said something about "finding me" as a child. That's the phrase she used, "when we found you."

I'm not genius on human reproduction, but most people "have" babies or "adopt" babies. They don't just "find" them.

But Brenda Hill insists I didn't hear her right. Sure, she's got a valid argument. My hearing isn't super, thanks to my thing. You never just have face blindness, you see. You have that plus something from a long ala cart menu of neurological issues. I suppose I'm fortunate. I have distorted hearing. I don't recognize voices. I can tell a man's from a woman's most of the time, but that's about it. Talking on the phone with anyone tends to be a challenge.

And people wonder why I'm not all that social.

What I really want to do is start questioning Mom again, but Kevin is waiting outside and I hate to take up more of his summer than I have to. I can't even say my driving lessons are helping him all that much because I'm pretty sure I'm not a good driver. At least, not in the most traditional definition of the term.

I grab my crutches and hoist myself off the settee. There's a good chance this cast weighs more than I do. I feel like I've got a cinder block wrapped around my leg. Mom opens the door for me and I step out into the sunny humidity.

"Hey, Kevin."

"Hey, Aunt Nora."

It takes me several awkward minutes to struggle down the five porch steps, hop/drag my cast across the four squares of concrete to the street where my almost twenty-year-old Forester is parked. I look at my beloved vehicle, with a critical eye. My literary agent, Connie, would be horrified if she saw what I'm driving.

Oh, yes. I'm an author. I write a series of pretty successful adventure books aimed at boys in junior high but the appeal of the books is pretty broad. And by pretty broad I mean when it comes to money…well, Connie would definitely be outraged that I'm still driving the car I got for my sixteenth birthday.

I tell myself I'm keeping the car because my father gave it to me. But it's also pretty likely I'm holding on to it to annoy everyone around me.

I'm funny like that.

Kevin opens the door for me, but thanks to the plaster tree stump I'm dragging I have to back into the seat and lift my leg in with my hands. So graceful.

"Where are we going today?" Kevin asks, sticking the key into the ignition.

I frown at him. "No place until you push in the clutch."

"Oh right." He pushes the clutch, turns the key and the car lurches forward. I let out a little yelp when my leg jolts against the door. "Sorry, Aunt Nora."

Kevin doesn't say much, which I like. My sisters' other offspring seem like young children next to him, and I think he feels a certain sense of responsibility, being the oldest of the nieces and nephews. But, he's sixteen, which means any positive instincts are buried under several layers of resentment and rebellion. It's not a stretch to say I find a kindred spirit in him.

We're moving and I close my eyes. I'm not worried about the driving when we're moving. It's the stopping and starting the boy has trouble with. So as long as the car is in motion I can relax.

"So, now we're moving, where're we going?"

"Rochester Deli." I don't open my eyes. After five weeks of eating my mother's healthy cooking I am in need of a big, hearty Reuben sandwich. Lucky for me, the world's best Reuben is a fifteen minute drive away.

"That's in downtown Waukesha."

I don't open my eyes. "You're going to have to get used to driving there at some point. Suck it up and stay in your lane." I don't need to be looking to know the boy's driving with the lane line directly beneath the vehicle.

For people who don't know the area, downtown Waukesha is a bit of a maze. Some people who have lived in Waukesha for decades still avoid the historic district with its cobblestone streets, quirky art shops, and friendly business owners. Too bad for them. More Reuben sandwiches for me.

My phone buzzes and I startle. I almost forgot I had a phone. I don't need to read the display. There are maybe six people who have my number. Mom, Lily, and Rose are the first three, and none of them is likely to call me since I'm, you know, living here now. And it's unlikely Jack's forgiven me enough to call me or let Sam call me. So that leaves Connie, my agent.

Connie is also my self-appointed guardian angel. She may not realize it, but I know she activated the tracking on the phone she sent to replace the one I lost in my mother's garage. Of course my mother then found the old phone…and used it…to call Jack and Connie thereby connecting all the fragile relationships I've managed to cultivate and keep very, very separate.

I was less than happy about that.

I swipe the screen and answer. "Hey Connie."

"Oh thank goodness! You're alive!" Connie wheezes.

"You sound out of breath. Have you been jogging?" I'm kidding, of course. Connie is always joining some exercise group or fitness class but it's pointless because while she knows she's…fluffy…she doesn't have the interest or the patience to actually participate in any form of organized exercise. The last group she joined was a step aerobics class for women over forty. They kicked Connie out because, and this is exactly what she told me they said, "swaying back and forth to the music while yelling at clients on the phone is not an aerobic work-out."

Believe me, Connie had plenty of ammunition loaded up ready to debate that point. But she realized it's hard to be taken seriously when you've squeezed a size 22 body into a size 12 spandex leotard and tried to cover everything with a giant t-shirt that screams "WAKE ME UP FOR DONUTS!"

Today Connie sounds breathless, like she's taking a stab at exercise again. "Oh yeah. I've been jogging. Haven't you heard? I'm training for a 5K."

I have trouble differentiating between serious tones and sarcasm sometimes, so for a second I believe Connie is telling me the truth. "Really?"

"No, of course not. The only thing 5K means to me is the number of words you've sent me in, oh, I don't know, the last eon. And you haven't moved in weeks. At first I thought you were just camping, like you do. But then I thought maybe you finally fell in some hole and died."

Clearly she's been talking to my mother often enough to have picked up on the whole "dead in a ditch" scenario. I would make a mental note to hate that fact, but I'm focused on something far more entertaining at the moment. "Connie, you are so busted!"

"What are you talking about?" Now Connie's using what I think is her innocent voice.

Because my hearing is distorted, I don't generally pick up on sarcasm or fake tones. This used to cause me all kinds of trouble when I was younger. I would take what anyone said as the plain truth. I'm far more cynical now. Unless it's my sister Rose, who has zero sense of humor and therefore speaks nothing but the flat truth, I assume whatever I hear is sarcasm or lies.

I realize that sounds awful. The truth is, I'm rarely wrong with that assumption.

Back to Connie. "Don't play innocent. I've always suspected you activated the tracking GPS on this phone before you shipped it to me."

"I did no such thing."

Her tone, over the phone, means little to my brain, but her words register as righteous indignation. Well, righteous indignation covering a lie. "Then how do you know my phone hasn't moved?" I generally reserve my attempts at a sugary sweet tone when I'm trying to escape one of my mother's endless discussions about bran. But if I can't get Brenda Hill to answer my questions about my earliest years, then at the very least I'm going to get my agent to admit she's been tracking my every move.

Connie is a captain of her industry. That's why she's my agent. She thinks outside the box, she has to, with me. We've never met in person. I only know she battles with her weight because, well, she tells me about it all the time and also she emails me pictures of herself with some other author she represents, smiling and pressing the flesh at a book signing.

I refuse to do book signings. Forget the fact that I really do not like being around people, I'm protecting Connie from…well, from me. If she caught a glimpse of my hair (often dyed a color not found in nature), fifteen…no, sixteen tattoos, and my multiple ear and eyebrow piercings she would run away screaming.

But I digress. Which is fine, since the other end of the line is silent because Connie has no retort for my question and we both know that the next person to speak, is going to lose this argument.

I make it a point not to lose arguments.

"Fine. You got me. Do you blame me? I've got a vested interest in your well being and you, my star client, like to go off in the woods and live like an animal for weeks on end without human contact. If you one day burn your face off in a campfire or fall off a mountain or something, I need to know."

"Connie, there are no mountains in Wisconsin."

"You don't always just stay in Wisconsin."

"And you'd only know that if you were tracking me."

But she has a valid concern. I tend to wander, and not like most people who meander through malls or museums. No, I wander across county lines, and yes, I've been known to drive aimlessly for hundreds of miles without really paying attention. Having face blindness creates all manner of awkward situations, and Connie, dear Connie, is usually the one who has to bail me out. I mean that literally. I've been arrested a couple of times.

"Look, Nora, it's not like I can control what you do. But I do have the right to know where my star client is."

I don't rise to do battle with her over this point because we've fought about this before. "Fine, but Connie, I'm at home. With my mother. I mean, I can't be much safer than that."

"Which reminds me: I got another thank you note from her. From your mom. Tell me again why she thinks I'm your caregiver?"

Oh, right. Yes, my family thinks my face blindness makes me some kind of mental invalid. When Mom called Connie on my lost phone she made the assumption that Connie's my personal caregiver. I guess Mom talked so much Connie didn't get a word in, which is really saying something given how rapid fire my agent can be with questions. I haven't gotten around to setting Mom straight. My family would never believe that I'm independently wealthy because of the books I write. So it's just easier for everyone, including Connie, though she doesn't know it, to think I have a caregiver who manages me.

Things would be different if my father were still alive. He understood me like no one else.

Well, I mean, until I reconnected with Jack.

Nope, not going to think about Jack right now. Not thinking about him and not answering any questions that will entangle me in a deeper conversation. Kevin's just made the turn onto South Street and we are a block away from the deli. I am going to focus on something good. Like getting a Reuben sandwich in my face.

So I divert the conversation.

"Connie, I'll have pages for you soon, I promise. It's just that I'm…" I want to say that I'm being slowly smothered in my mother's temple of perfection. She has white furniture. I use semi-permanent hair color…a lot. It's not a good combo.

Connie doesn't question the switch in gears. "So you'll drop those pages off when you show up for the book signing?"

I must have growled or something because Kevin takes his attention off of his seventh attempt at parallel parking to stare at me. I try to be as polite as possible, but Connie knows my feelings about public appearances all too well. "If I wanted to be put on display, I'd have gone into a different line of work, like maybe modeling."

"So you're saying you could be a model?"

I know Connie's fishing for what I look like. It kills her, not knowing everything about me. I'll admit, I take a certain amount of pleasure in tormenting her. "Oh sure, I can do sad, underfed, and pale." It's not a stretch. I just can't do tall. My sisters are tall. My mother is tall. I feel like I'm standing in a hole when I'm next to them.

"You know book sales do better when readers have a connection with the author."

"Well that's not true. Book sales do better when the book is good."

"Or if it's written by a celebrity."

We both laugh. Connie might be a shameless money chaser, but she does have standards. In the past she has turned down huge contracts because she refuses to rep semi-literate celebrities who think their biography is worth reading. I respect her for that and I trust her with my career.

Just not with the bigger issues in my life. I don't trust anyone with that.

Well, except maybe Jack.

Nope. Not going there. Time to change the subject. "Connie I have to run. My nephew's about to put a hole in my tire if he hits the curb one more time." Now that Connie knows I wasn't spawned by wolves, I've shared a few details about my family. She knows I'm teaching Kevin to drive, although she has no idea it's because I can't drive my car myself. If she knew about the broken leg and foot, she'd probably swoop in with an army of doctors to make sure I was taking care of myself.

Oh and she doesn't know about the whole, "when we found you" thing. No one's going to learn about that until I get an answer from good old Brenda Hill. And Brenda is not talking.

I end the call and realize Kevin is staring at me. We are perfectly parked in a small surface parking lot a block away from the Rochester Deli. While I was talking to Connie, Kevin gave up parallel parking and found a spot. I sense he's annoyed with me.

"I would never put a hole in your tire, Aunt Nora."

"I know."

"I don't even think they test for parallel parking anymore anyway. I was just trying it to see if I could get closer to the deli so you didn't have to walk so far on your crutches."

Have I mentioned he's a good kid? "I know."

"Then why were you bad mouthing me to..." he stops because he's suddenly less interested in being indignant and more interested in what he overheard. "You're sending pages to someone? What, like a book or something?"

"Or something." I open the car door and begin the unloading process. Thank goodness my car is a little taller than some and I don't have to hoist myself from three inches off the ground to get out. Although, pulling myself up from a sitting position and then balancing on one foot while I retrieve the crutches from the back seat has been a pretty good body building regimen.

Look at me, I'm a weight lifter.

Kevin gets out on his side and helps me free the crutches. "So what, you write books and send them to that person you were talking to and they get published?"

"Can we just go to the deli? I'm hungry."

I know, I'm a hypocrite. I'm not answering Kevin's question just like I'm not getting answers from Mom. But guess what? I smell corned beef and so I do not care.

The Rochester Deli is a small place attached to an equally small and equally delicious bakery. We place our order with the young man at the front counter and find a table. Since it's pretty late for lunch, the place isn't

24

crowded, which is just how I like it. Nice and quiet and free of faces that will only serve to confuse and annoy me.

"Seventy-six!" A moderately heavy-set girl comes to the window and shouts our number. Kevin doesn't make me get up, because he's a good kid, so he fetches our food. While he's walking back I catch a look at the girl in the delivery window.

My head starts pounding and everything begins to get fuzzy.

I try to blink away the black-out I sense is coming. I simply do not have the time or the patience for this.

I look at the girl again and realize she's no girl, and she's not really so much heavy set as she is pregnant. She can't be much younger than I am. I'm relieved. I'm not getting that black out feeling over her.

I look at my food and feel optimistic. Maybe I'm not sensing some impending missing child. Maybe my brain is wonky because of my broken leg. Everything is out of balance. I'm just getting that headache and black out feeling because I'm out of whack.

Yes. I like that theory. That theory means I can ignore the warning signs and enjoy my Reuben.

But I can't leave it alone. I have to know the girl's age. Then I'll feel better. "Kevin, that girl that just handed you the food…how old is she?"

Kevin glances over his shoulder and then back at me. "You know her, Aunt Nora. That's Cassie Wilson. She's married to Casper Wilson over at church? They're greeters. You've said good morning to them every Sunday since you've been staying with Grandma."

Kevin understands I have a thing about faces, but he hasn't quite grasped what that means in the real world.

My headache is getting worse. I try breathing slowly to avoid fainting in a public place. Not that I haven't done that before, but it's not exactly something I'm proud of. Right now I'm more confused than anything else. I'm having the headache and the black-out feelings…but there's no kid involved.

See, I have this thing, not the face blindness, it's another thing, and I can't escape it. Some people call it a talent, some a gift, I just think of it as yet another thing I have that makes my life a challenge. I'm able to find missing children, especially the ones who are in imminent danger of death or some sort of destruction.

Now, sure, probably lots of people have this ability. I mean, who doesn't want to help kids? And don't get me wrong, I like helping kids. It's just that the way it happens for me is so weird, so…otherworldly…that people have a hard time believing it.

Personally, I think this is just another joke God's played on me. It's like God came down to me one day and said, "Hey there Nora, you know how you can't recognize faces, not even your own? Well we're going to top that off by making you someone who finds missing children when no one else can because you have a vision or hear a voice or something equally unprovable. Sure, there will be those who suspect you're the one to kidnap or harm the child in the first place and they'll want to arrest you and throw you in jail. Just think of that as part of this nifty little game you humans call life." And now I get headaches and black out

26

when I come in some kind of contact with a child I'm supposed to find.

Really screws up my day, let me tell you.

But this is odd, even for me. I look around the deli, there are no children anywhere. There's no TV reporting a missing child, no radio. No one's even on their phones. Just a couple people eating lovely sandwiches, much like the one that's getting cold in front of me. Yet here I am, with a blazing headache, looking at a woman in her twenties, and wondering if my "gift" just expanded to adults or if my mental wires are completely crossed.

I suppose it could just be a regular old headache.

But we all know it's not.

"She's pretty old, I think, like maybe twenty-six or something. And she's gotten kind of fat since she's been pregnant."

I blink in Kevin's general direction. I'd love to laugh at his innocent idea of what is considered old. If twenty-six is old in his eyes then I must be ancient at thirty-three and my mother must be a positive dinosaur. Kids are funny.

And rude. That last crack about Cassie was rude. I need to correct him on it. A good aunt would.

But I can't dwell on silly things like manners at the moment. I'm getting the message that someone in this room is facing calamity, but there's no clear picture as to who that person might be. So I have to try and sort this out and the only way to do that is to make some kind of closer contact with Cassie. I struggle to my feet, ignoring the look I'm getting from my nephew as I crutch myself over to the window.

A pregnant lady comes up to the order window. Now, since Cassie's been out of my sight for a couple minutes I haven't a clue if this person in front of me is the same person I saw three minutes ago.

Isn't my life super fun?

"Cassie?"

"Yes? Oh, Nora! Hi!"

That's where my social skills end. Now what do I say? "I thought it was you. I just wanted to say...hi. So, hi."

"Oh aren't you so nice? Well thanks for stopping in and enjoy your lunch!" Cassie reaches out and touches my shoulder.

And the room goes black.

FRIDAY, 3:30 PM

The thing about passing out in public is that the people around you tend to freak out. I'm used to my black outs. But, given my general avoidance of humans, there aren't many who have witnessed a fainting spell. Which is why, when I open my eyes, the first thing I see is my mother's face.

This raises a number of questions, the biggest one being, "Just how long was I out this time?" My blackouts can range in time from a barely noticeable blink to a much larger gap in time, sometimes up to an hour. I've not yet been able to figure out the connection between the length of time I'm unconscious and the danger level to the kid I'm supposed to find.

Which brings me to a general question I've had for a long time: Why is it every kid that goes missing has some kind of death clock on them? This summer alone I've had to track down a girl with deadly asthma and no rescue inhaler and a boy with a really rare pain syndrome and massive internal bleeding. It seems like I get these assignments from the Divine Being who enjoys messing with me. And every time there's always some kind of countdown to death if I don't move quickly enough.

Puts a lot of pressure on a girl.

I manage to sit up, with a lot of help from Kevin and Cassie. Cassie's touch on my arm makes the room spin again. There's a definite connection between my finding kids thing and Cassie Wilson. But she's no kid and she's clearly not missing.

This is about the time I could use Jack's calm energy. Or maybe some of Sam's never ending cheerfulness. Or both.

Nope. It's not an option for me to think about them. Jack made it abundantly clear that I was no good for him or for Sam.

Any mystery that needs solving is going to be all on me.

"Eleanor, you had us all worried!" My mother flutters around like some geriatric flapper girl while Cassie and Kevin hoist me into a chair.

I hate it when she calls me Eleanor. I mean, yes, it's my name. But man, did my parents drop the ball when they named me. See, Lily's real name is Sussana, but the Biblical meaning is "Lily." And Rose's real name, also from the Bible, is Rhoda, but it means Rose. Beautiful, poetic, Biblical names. Me, I got named after my Grandma Hill. And guess what Eleanor means?

Well, okay, I've never actually looked it up. But that's beside the point. Since I was eight I've insisted people call me "Nora." And everyone does, except my mother.

"Mom, I'm fine. I just got a little dizzy."

"A little dizzy? No way dude, you were out cold! You took a header right into the ice tea dispenser."

Well at least Kevin's explained why my hair and shirt are wet. But I'm not exactly appreciating his honesty at the moment.

"Are you okay, Nora?" Cassie puts her hand on my shoulder. AgainI have to blink hard to keep everything in focus.

"Cassie, how old are you?"

Admittedly this is an odd question from someone emerging from a faint covered in ice tea, but I've never been one to follow all the social niceties.

Cassie gives me a weak smile. "I'm twenty-six. Why?"

"Oh, no reason." I try to be funny, which never works for me. "I just like to keep track of the people I faint on."

30

"That's enough right now Eleanor, we are taking you to the doctor." Brenda Hill is trying to take control of the situation.

I should probably go. But I hate, hate, hate doctors. It's a feeling that goes back to my grade school years when my parents took me to every emergency room, urgent care clinic, and faith healer trying to figure out why I would descend into tearful screams every time a relative tried to hug me. Either I was being willfully naughty or I was violently ill. My mother, mindful of all social manners, was convinced it was a violent illness that kept me from behaving politely. She wasn't completely disappointed when, after years of poking and prodding and all manner of archaic testing, one of those medical professionals figured out my thing and gave it a name. After that, Mom would cover for my social gaffs by whispering, "Well, you know she has prosopagnosia." People would nod as if they totally got it and I was given a pass.

While I'm pondering my medical past, I don't even realize that Kevin and Mom have walked me out of the deli and halfway to the car. Oh, and all without my sandwich!

So I guess this is happening. I'm going to a doctor.

FRIDAY 4:00 PM

My brain is sort of like a long hallway with doors on either side. I shove my unpleasant memories or experiences behind one of those doors and lock it tightly, never to be opened again. This is what I'm trying to do right now. Here I am stuck in my car while my mother, sitting in the back seat, yammers on about my mental condition. We could have taken Mom's car, but she decided today was the day

31

she was taking a car load of her hoarder nonsense to Goodwill, thus filling every nook and cranny in her car with stuff.

She better not chicken out about getting rid of it when we get home.

Meanwhile, Kevin muscles his way through traffic. I honestly believe he's hitting every pothole and short stopping at every light on purpose. I'll blame my headache on the less than comfortable ride, but I know very well that's not why my head hurts.

I'm never quite sure if God's the one sending me these assignments or what, but it simplifies my life to believe He is. If there's someone other than the Almighty jogging my noggin I just as soon not know.

Cassie Wilson is not a child and she's not missing. Now, granted, I've wound up hunting for kids before that didn't start out missing, but wound up that way. Kids are sort of slippery like that.

"I just don't know why you can't take better care of yourself, Eleanor."

These are the first words in my mother's stream of conscious monologue that I'm hearing, though I'm aware she's been talking in my general direction for the past fifteen minutes. Kevin, miraculously, has managed to get us to the door of the urgent care center in one piece.

But I can't let this comment go unnoticed. "Mom, I do take care of myself. I just don't chose to go see a doctor any old time I have an ache and a pain."

"Nora, you passed out in a deli. You are covered in iced tea. That's more than an ache and a pain."

Not quite sure which part of that is a bigger issue for Mom. She hates messes, and when I was little I was constantly getting covered in something; food, mud, dog slobber, whatever. I am a magnet for mess. So the iced tea is probably putting her on edge more than the black out.

"Yeah, Aunt Nora, that was scary the way you just fell over sideways."

"No one asked you, Kevin." I can't help but snarl at the poor kid. He's in the middle of a battle he didn't start and probably doesn't even know is going on. I should feel more sympathy, but at this moment, as I'm being guided through the sliding doors of a medical facility, I'm doing all I can to keep the door in my brain tightly locked.

Kevin runs and grabs a wheelchair. They load me into the wheelchair and I'm now powerless to stop forward motion. We get into the building and are stopped at the check in desk because there's a line.

My cell buzzes in my pocket. It doesn't even matter who's trying to reach me. It could be a telemarketer selling time shares in Death Valley. Whatever it is, I'm going to make this a very long phone call and delay actually going in to an exam room.

I look at the display.

Sam's calling me. She's making an actual phone call.

This must be important.

"Sorry guys, I have to take this." I nod to Kevin to push me out of line and into a spot where I can be out of the way. I wave Kevin off and give my mother the biggest glare

I can muster. Once I'm confident I'm out of earshot, I answer. "Hey there Sam. What's up?"

"Nora," her voice is a low whisper. "I need to talk to you."

"Okay, fire away."

There's a pause and some muffled conversation. Then she comes back. "That fight you and Dad had, what was it really about?"

Leave it to Sam to ask the world's most difficult questions. "I think your Dad is just trying to protect you and he thought I wasn't probably the most responsible person in the world."

"Yeah, well, I wish you would talk to him."

The hair on the back of my neck stands up. "What's going on?"

"I heard him talking to my uncle this morning and he's talking about selling the shop and moving to work with my uncle."

"That doesn't sound like such a bad thing. Where would you be moving?"

"St. Louis."

The doors in my brain all begin to rattle at once. The noise is deafening. St. Louis. Why did it have to be there? In all the times I've been sent or directed or whatever to find a missing child, St. Louis was the only time I was too late. And I've locked that memory deep, deep, deep down at the end of my mind's hallway behind heavy locks.

Sam doesn't know this. Jack doesn't know this. No one knows about St. Louis other than me.

I take a deep breath. I have to keep steady for Sam's sake. This might be a great move for Jack. Without knowing all the facts, I might say the wrong thing and drive a wedge between father and daughter, and I won't do that. I hold that relationship as sacred. "Sam, I'm sure if you guys do move, it's for the best."

There's a long pause on her end of the phone. "Dad called you, didn't he? He called you and told you to tell me this was for the best!"

Before I can say one more word, she hangs up and I'm left sitting there in my wheelchair, staring at my phone. Of course Jack hasn't called me. Jack isn't speaking to me as far as I know and probably for this very reason.

Jack's been a single parent since the day Sam was born. Sam's mother had no interest in even having a baby after a college party hook-up, but Jack stepped up to his responsibility. Mr. All American lost his football scholarship and every dime he had, but he convinced the woman to give birth instead of getting an abortion. After Sam was born, Jack returned to Manitowoc, hoping his parents would help him with the baby, but that was not to be. As far as I'm aware, Jack hasn't spoken to his parents in the fourteen years since he brought Sam home, and they don't live more than three miles apart.

Makes my relationship with my family look down-right dreamy.

If Jack's thinking about moving, it's because the car repair shop he owns isn't doing great and he's looking for a better life for Sam. I have my doubts about the move to St.

Louis. I mean, my issues aside, St. Louis isn't exactly as family friendly as Manitowoc.

I'm tempted to just write a huge check that would bail Jack out of whatever problems he's got. I could do that. I have more money than I'm ever going to need and if I tried to give it to my family they'd be convinced I stole it or something. The temptation to do that is huge, but I'm sure if I do, I'd be interfering with his parenting, which is pretty much what we fought about that day in Superior. I don't know everything, I certainly don't know Jack's perspective, so maybe it's not financial and he just wants to get as far away from me as he can.

Either way, I need to stay out of it until I'm invited in.

I look up and see two people I know to be Kevin and my mother...mostly because I remember Kevin's wearing a Milwaukee Brewers baseball jersey and my mother is wearing her favorite yellow blouse. If that woman every gets a new favorite blouse, I'm doomed because I won't be able to pick her out in a crowd. I know they want to wheel me back to the waiting line so some doctor can treat me like a science experiment, but I have no interest in making them feel better anymore. I've got two mysteries on my hands now and I need to be alone to think.

"Okay, let's go dear. We're checked in."

I shake my head at my mother's words. "I can't do it, Mom. I have other things I need to do."

"Like what? What is more important than your health?"

Well, I'd explain that my health isn't at risk just because I blacked out, but then I'd have to explain the blackouts and how I find lost children and all of that and frankly, I don't think she has the capacity to fully understand it all. That's not a knock on her. I don't have the capacity to fully understand it all and I'm the one living the life.

"That call was pretty important. It was about…a friend. A friend who needs some help." It's not a lie. I'm sure Jack needs plenty of help dealing with a cranky teen who doesn't want to move to another state. He just doesn't need my help.

"You have a friend?" My mother's face brightens in a way that breaks my heart a little. I forget, sometimes, that in spite of our fights and our views on life and in spite of how different we are, she still loves me and just wants the best for me. The fact that I mention having a friend probably opened the heavens and she can hear the angels singing.

"Yes, I do. You know her. Sam? Jack's daughter? You talked to Jack when I was in Superior?"

Mom's face clouds. "Right. Your friend is a thirteen year old girl."

"She's fourteen." Not that clarifying Sam's age makes me seem any less of a loser.

"Is she cute?" Kevin has to know.

Honestly, the kid says like five words a day and half of them make me want to roll on the floor laughing. "She's cute enough, I guess." But how would I know? It's not like I remember what she looks like. "Anyway, she's got a problem and wanted to talk to me about it."

"Does she live around here?"

"No, she doesn't, and now it looks like she's moving even farther way, so just, you know, find a girl in your own town."

"And maybe you could find a friend your own age, Nora." My mother looks straight ahead. I can't see her face and her tone of voice lost on me. But there's no hiding the fact that she's disappointed that I think of Sam, rather than Jack, as my friend.

I've got too much other stuff to deal with at the moment. "I have to make a couple of phone calls and honestly, I don't have time to sit here and wait anymore. Can we just get me back to the car so I can get on with things?"

"Nora, in the time you've wasted talking to some child we could have been seen by a doctor."

Is anyone else's mom like this? I've heard that "in the time we've been doing this…" line maybe ten thousand times and it never ceases to annoy me. I get it. Sure, by now I probably would have seen a doctor, although what good that would do is beyond me) but I have priorities and while they are not your priorities at this moment, Mom, they are important to me.

Because I get to call Jack and talk to him.

Although, maybe I shouldn't get involved. Maybe I should just let them move away to a city I'll never ever go to because I can't even say the name of it out loud without getting nauseous. That would be the smart thing to do.

But of all the things I am, smart might not be one of them.

"Look, I have errands to deal with. Isn't that why we were out in the first place?"

"But you fainted, dear. You need medical attention."

"Mom, I'm fine, honestly." I'd tell her I do this all the time, but I sense I have her mentally giving up and I don't want to wreck my chance. "I feel great. I think I just got up too fast or something, you know how stuff like that can happen."

"That's true, Grandma. I read once where people can stand up too fast and faint because the blood rushes to their heads too fast…or does the blood not rush up to their heads fast enough?" Kevin is standing behind me, ready to push me out the door, but if that kid looks half as perplexed as he sounds, we're in trouble.

My mother frowns, then sighs. I know that sigh. I'm the reason she has that sigh. She's lost another round with me. "Fine, Nora. We'll go. Just get me back to my car and you can get on with your errands."

I fight the urge to give Kevin a high five as we wheel out of the clinic.

FRIDAY 5:30 PM

Having not eaten my lovely Reuben at the Rochester Deli, I'm wildly hungry but my mind is too occupied to let my stomach dictate terms. I let Kevin have free reign of the car, driving wherever he desires, with the understanding that he must do so in complete silence and without getting either of us killed.

I'm not saying that my mental wrestling over whether or not to call Jack is as epic as Jacob wrestling with God (although I have a leg injury, so there's that parallel) but it does take me several minutes to decide that yes, I do need to jump in and get nosy. I stare at Jack's number in my phone and wonder why I bothered to add it to my short list of contacts. I really don't need to store numbers. In yet another fun mental quirk I'm able to memorize any phone number simply by seeing it once. Don't think the irony is lost on me. The girl who can't recognize a face she's seen ten thousand times can dial a phone number she saw once ten years ago.

Which is not to say I don't have any stored contacts, I do. Sam grabbed my phone recently and put her information in there, and Connie insists I have her number stored. Just to keep the peace in the family I've got my mom's and sisters' numbers saved although I never call them. Somehow it makes them feel safe knowing their information is locked away in a cell phone I often forget I have. The only other number I keep is that of Golden Chicken in Waukesha, home of the finest fried chicken in Southeastern Wisconsin.

Now I'm hungry for chicken.

Forcing myself to focus, I dial Jack and wait for him to answer. And wait, and wait.

I get voicemail.

Oh what am I going to say? "Hey, your kid called me and wants me to change your mind about moving to a city I'm afraid of even though you told me in no uncertain terms I'm a bad influence on her and you can't have me around?"

Yeah, that sounds good. Let's go with that.

"Hey, Jack…it's Nora." I'm really hoping the weak little girl voice is the result of my distorted hearing and not how I really sound. "So Sam called me a little bit ago. She seems…she seems worried about something. Maybe give me a call if you have a minute?"

I end the call. Kevin is staring at me. "Kevin, get your eyes on the road."

"We're in a parking lot, Aunt Nora."

I look out the window. The kid is right. We're in a parking lot. And not just any lot, we are parked smack dab in front of Golden Chicken.

"Kevin, why are we here?"

"You said you wanted chicken."

I did? Have I started talking out loud without knowing I'm talking out loud?

Boy, if I start doing that, we're all doomed. I can't have people knowing what's really in my head.

But as long as we're here and I'm hungry, I may as well pick up dinner.

FRIDAY, 6:00 PM

Golden Chicken cranks out the best fried chicken, no question. But it is not a place where you'd want to spend quality time, especially in the summer. This tiny space is overwhelmed by the steamy heat from the kitchen filling the air. It's really not an eatery in the sense that you're not going to eat dinner there. They deliver or you can pick up, but there's no lingering at Golden Chicken. There are also no credit cards allowed, it's all cash or checks. So, in a move my father would denounce as lazy and antisocial, I place an order by phone in spite of the fact I'm sitting nine feet from the cook line.

I wait the prescribed thirty minutes in the air conditioned comfort of the Forester. Kevin is blissfully buried in social media so we spend the time side by side in silence. Just the way I like it.

Late August is a humid time in Southeastern Wisconsin, with the moisture in the air clinging to clothing. It feels like I'm breathing in warm water as I struggle to get myself and the crutches out of the car and up to the check out counter.

Why didn't I send Kevin on this errand?

Good question. Chalk it up to the fact that I was antsy and needed to move, or maybe I'm a little tired of being helpless. Or maybe I'm just a nice auntie who figured the kid could use a break for a minute. Anyway, fifteen seconds after leaving the car, I regret my decision to fetch the steaming bags of fried goods. I get as far as the screen door, and I know I'm not going to manage this. I wave at Kevin who gets out of the car and leaves the drivers' door wide open, letting out all the cool air. Annoying, but better than closing the door and locking the car keys in there. I hand him the money and hobble back to the Forester.

In the time it takes me to get situated in my seat, Kevin returns with the food. He looks a little goggled at the amount of chicken he's carrying, but hey, I figure if I drive home and Mom hasn't eaten yet or if one of the sisters is over there with her gaggle of kids, then I'll be a little bit of a hero. And who doesn't like that feeling?

This is when I notice the glove box is open…and the small, sealed urn containing my portion of my father's ashes isn't there.

When my father died Mother opted to have him cremated and then divided four ways . Mom and my sisters keep their portions of Dad in lovely silver boxes on their mantles. Each year they have a fun little polishing party where they get together and chit chat and polish those silver boxes while Dad's remains sit in small industrial grade plastic bags on the dining room table.

That doesn't sound very restful to me. My share of my father is with me all the time, in my glove box, in a sealed box. On my travels I look for the perfect place to leave his ashes. So far, in the fifteen years I've been looking, I haven't found the right place. So he stays in my car. It comforts me to know that a part of him is always with me.

But it's not something I share with the rest of my tribe. If I did, I'm sure the matriarchs would be shocked to the point of demanding I give them my piece of Dad to put in their little silver boxes. And I'm not going to do that.

So it's a bit disturbing that someone, and by someone I mean Kevin, has been rustling around in my glove box and has discovered where I'm keeping Dad. Panic grips me as I twist around in my seat, hoping the urn freed itself of the glove box and is currently sunning itself next to one of the car windows.

Anything, no matter how ridiculous, is preferable to my mother and sisters finding out I carry that urn in my car.

"Wow, this is some good smelling chicken!" Kevin sets the aromatic packages in the back seat before getting behind the wheel again.

"Kevin? Buddy?"

He turns blankly innocent eyes to me. "Yeah?"

"Where is it?"

He blinks those same innocent eyes. "Where is what?"

I bite my lip. I can't lose my temper with the kid. He's my only source of anything resembling freedom. "You were in my glove box."

"Right. I was looking for a pen."

Well that's not true. Kevin is attached to his phone. It's an extension of his hand. And I know there's a note taking app for his phone. "A pen? Really? When was the last time you wrote anything with a pen? You type everything into that phone of yours!"

"Why are you getting so steamed, Aunt Nora?"

"Because my—because something important is missing."

"Was it that metal vase thing?"

I nod and blink. I'm trying to fight back unexpected tears. It's like losing my father all over again. All this time I've been waiting for the right moment and the right place to lay his ashes to rest and now here this kid rips through my life and loses my last piece of my beloved Dad.

"Oh, it must've fallen…" he reaches between the seats. "Here it is. I'm sorry, Aunt Nora. I really was looking for a pen. I wanted to write down the address of this place… and phone number. In case I ever want to…you know, order chicken."

"Why didn't you just put it in your phone? Why did you have to go digging through my stuff?" Even to my distorted sense of hearing, I know I'm yelling.

He blinks again, and I'm almost afraid he's going to cry…and then he heaves a sigh. "Okay, I wasn't going to write down the phone number. I thought of a cool idea for a tattoo and I wanted to sketch it on my arm, to see what it looked like."

"You…wait…what?" If the kid had told me he wanted to shave his head and learn to ballroom dance he couldn't have shocked me more.

"You promise you won't tell Mom?"

This could be good. I mean, the kid is already at my bidding because I let him drive my car. But at some point he's going to get his license and then he won't need me and I might still need him. Who knows how long I'll really be weighted down with this cast? A little leverage against him is not a bad thing. "I promise. As long as it's not something illegal."

"It's not. I promise it's not. I like coming up with ideas for tattoos. See, I've always thought yours were cool and I, um, I sort of…"

"Oh Kevin spit it out!"

"Okay. I want to be a tattoo artist when I grow up. But I want to do like religious tattoos, like yours. I don't want to do anything dirty or wrong, you know?"

I rub my temples in a weak attempt to keep from laughing out loud. "So, you want to be a Christian tattoo artist?"

"Yeah. Exactly. And I get these ideas all the time and I sketch them out so that when I open my own shop I have all kinds of things for people to choose from. But you can't tell Mom."

No. I can't. I'm fairly certain something deep inside Rose would rupture if she knew what her eldest wanted to do with his life. Hey, I would love to have a place I can go to get a new tattoo that doesn't make me feel like I've jumped to the dark side. Besides, the kid's only sixteen. By the time he's ready to go to college, who knows what he'll want to do. I know Rose plans on him being an orthodontist.

Wouldn't this be a kick if he went through with it?

Kids are funny.

"Okay, Kevin, I'll keep your secret. But you cannot, seriously you cannot, go digging around in my stuff." I take the urn from his hand and put it back in the glove box.

"So is that thing what I think it is? It looks like one of the urns Billy Lane got when his great grandma died.

Everyone in the family got like this little urn of her ashes. Billy keeps his in his locker and tells freshmen if he throws it at them and it hits them, then they're cursed by his dead grandma."

"Billy Lane is a pig."

"Yeah. So, is that Grandpa Hill?"

What, I'm going to lie to the kid after he tells me his secret? "Yeah."

"Dude, you haven't buried that anyplace yet? Mom said you buried it back when you were in high school?"

Oh like I would ever leave my father where I went to high school. Nothing good came out of that town.

Well, except that's where I met Jack.

Getting off topic. "No, I haven't found the right place for him, yet. But your mom and Aunt Lily and Grandma wouldn't like it if they knew I still had this in my car."

"So I guess we're keeping each other's secrets?" He grins at me.

"Yeah, yeah. Can we get home now? The chicken's getting cold."

"Can I stay at Grandma's for dinner? I've never had Golden Chicken."

"Of course."

I'm not surprised he's not familiar with Golden Chicken. My sisters don't, what's the word, tolerate anything that even sniffs of junk food. I was at Rose's house one night for dinner and she presented everyone with a salad laced with quinoa. And that was it. No meat, no eggs, no anything with flavor. Salad and quinoa, if that's even food, that's what she gave us.

She says it's to keep everyone trim and healthy. Well, I weigh about ninety pounds, and that's if I've got my heavy coat and hiking boots on. So I pass on quinoa, thank you, and take friend chicken every time.

"I'm guessing you want to stay at Grandma's for dinner then?"

Kevin eases out of our parking space and nods. "If I can."

And just like, with Kevin knowing one of my secrets, I have yet another person wedging into the inner circle of my life. It's getting crowded in here. I cross my arms and we ride back home in silence.

Even past six it's plenty hot and humid. The only real good news is that the mosquitoes have been light this year. That fact means little to people outside the Upper Midwest, but we're thankful for a break from those blood sucking bugs. As we pull up to my mother's house I see Brenda sitting on the front porch, fanning herself. I know it's her because no one else would be willingly sitting outside in this kind of energy draining weather. My mother is not a fan of heat and humidity, but she also hates paying for air conditioning so in the evenings sometimes she'll open all the windows and then sit on the front porch. Then, before she goes to bed, she'll close up all the windows again and turn on the AC, which has to work harder because the hot has heated up. I've tried to explain to her that if she just leaves the house closed, the AC won't have to work as hard and her bill might actually be lower. She doesn't see my point.

Everyone else in the family treats this as normal behavior. But I guess everyone else's definition of normal is different from mine so I've given up arguing.

"Hey Mom," I puff and pant as I'm dragging my cemented leg up the short flight of porch stairs. "We brought dinner. I figured you didn't want to heat up the house."

"Oh that's so nice, Nora. I was going to go over to Lily's tonight, but then I heard she was making something involving tofu and I decided to pass. Tofu gives me gas," she adds, as if I didn't know.

Sometimes she and I understand each other perfectly. It's rare so I sit in the white wicker chair next to her and revel in the moment.

She sighs heavily. "Tomorrow there's a funeral at church I have to sing for."

"Who's funeral?"

She shrugs, "Jennifer Turley. She went to hospice last week and it didn't take long." It's not like Mrs. Turley and my mom are close. In fact, the only thing they had in common was that church. Mom's been a member at the same church for almost twenty years, and she volunteers all the time. When she's not baking something for a church function or cleaning up the yard or the flower beds or covering tables in the fellowship hall for some food centric event, she's singing in any one of three choirs or helping the pastors with something or another.

The thing is…I don't think she even likes that church. She just does it all because she was a minister's wife for so long, she doesn't know how to shut it off or quit one church and go to another.

I'm feeling magnanimous because of the tofu comment, so I make an offer I know I'm going to regret. "Want me to come with you?"

My mother couldn't smile bigger if I told her I was getting all my tattoos removed. "Oh Nora, that would be just lovely if you came along."

"Okay, what time is the funeral?"

"It's early, I believe nine tomorrow morning."

That is early, but what, I have something else pressing I can't show up and show some respect? I mean, I know that disaster generally follows me into and out of churches. Look at the last time I tried, I wound up plunging a dead mouse out of a toilet and fighting with Jack in the parking lot.

At the thought of Jack I pull my phone out of my pocket. What, like I thought he was actually going to call back?

Kevin announces he's set the table and dinner is served. I follow my mother into the stifling house and enjoy some fried chicken while trying to put Jack Terrell and his daughter and her phone call and Cassie Wilson and my black out all out of my head.

That's a lot to ask from a piece of fried chicken. Good thing I got extra fries.

SATURDAY 9:30 AM

I don't mind funerals because funerals aren't like regular church services. There's no looking around judging what each person is wearing or if the babies are quiet or if we're all awake and paying attention. And funerals are better than weddings because, let's be honest, the level of expectation for a funeral is far lower. That may sound cold and heartless, but I was raised to believe that a believer's death was actually a happy thing: that person was in Heaven having a blast with St. Peter and John the Baptist. (Honestly, I think would be fun to hang with John. I mean, he was the original outcast when it came to what I like to call the Dress Code of the Faithful. Camel's hair? And he ate bugs? Forget it, John the Baptist and I would be besties.) My father taught me that the only reason funerals are sad is because we are going to miss the person who died and so we are weeping for ourselves, and not for the person in the casket.

So when you're at a service for a really old person, like we are this morning, the congregation is sad-ish, but mostly just looking forward to the ham sandwiches and decorated cake in the fellowship hall later. Mom and I ride the elevator to the balcony and I land myself in the chair nearest the elevator doors. This is a chair typically reserved for the organist to use during the sermon, but too bad, so sad. Even Brenda understands we need to limit the amount of moving around I do, so as to limit the amount of chaos that can follow me.

I read the "in memoriam" the church secretary typed up. I count six typos. This is nice for me to notice because I was once the church secretary here and I was good at it. My mother thought it would be a great career for me, especially since it put me in front of various young vicars, youth pastors, and the occasional single deacon. Unfortunately for dear old Mom, my need for tattoos and multicolored hair made me a bad candidate for the buttoned up job, and an even worse candidate as a wife for that particular gaggle of ganders.

Still, nice to see they haven't replaced me with some perfectionist.

The service itself is a bit of a blur. I try to listen and get what God's saying about the death of this elderly follower of His, but I always come back to the same question: If God wants me in His house as His child, why oh why did He make it difficult for me to live in any society, especially one as small and close-knit as a church? I don't even recognize a picture of Jesus. How can I be a God's child when God made it impossible to even recognize a commonly accepted picture of Jesus? I've been asking since I got my diagnosis and one not even my father was able to answer completely.

Which would explain a big part of why I'm still searching for a spiritual home.

Mom wants to stay for the luncheon and I don't have a good reason not to stay. Besides, she's my ride. What, I'm going to walk home?

"Oh look, Nora, there's Cassie Wilson. You remember her from the Rochester Deli yesterday, right?"

I look over my shoulder, just to please Mom, because there's no way in the world I'm going to recognize Cassie Wilson right now. Turns out, she's serving sandwiches and cake to the mourners. She brings a tray of cold ham sandwiches to our table and as I take the tray from her, our hands brush. The tray slips out of my hands, fortunately falling onto the table. Not that there's anything I can do about it at the moment, I'm too busy trying very hard not to pass out.

There is no doubt in my mind that something is going to happen to Cassie and I'm going to be the one to have to track her down when it does happen. Apparently this gift of finding missing children, this gift I love so well, (get my sarcasm) has broadened and now adults who are clearing just fine and dandy are landing on my list.

Oh goodie.

My cell buzzes. I blink away the last of the dizziness, and look at the screen. It's Sam. I ignore the call. This is not the time or place for more angst. I need to clear my head and get ready for the next step in the whole "finding Cassie" process. Which means I need to listen for a quiet voice that's going to tell me where to find her.

A little too mystical for most people's tastes, but that's my life.

My mother chit-chats for almost half an hour before deciding she's been there long enough to satisfy the rules of church etiquette. Once inside the confines of the car, she rattles off a litany of complaints about this person and that person, all fine, upstanding church members who have said or done something she finds inexcusable. She relays how one of Lily's precious lambs was wronged by the demon spawn grandchild of another member and she, Brenda Hill, was just about at the end of her rope with it all.

Normally I ignore Mom when she's on a rant about church. When I was a kid her rants were directed toward Dad, who could absorb them with an easy grace. Since his passing, she's gotten more involved (if that's even possible) in the church and with more involvement comes more stories about people who just aren't doing Christianity right.

She seems really worked up for someone who just ate two pieces of decorated funeral cake, so I ignore my better judgement and ask a question. "Mom, if this church makes you so upset, why don't you just find one you like better?"

I know I've said something monumentally stupid. Mom takes a break in her constant stream of vocalizing to gather herself to squash a challenge she deems to be ridiculous. "Nora, I can't just leave that church. I've been a member there since your father died. All my friends are there."

"Well, you wouldn't know it to hear you talk."

I don't know why I say things. I should just be quiet.

"I wouldn't expect you to understand, given how you don't darken the door of a church unless someone forces you. I pray for you, Nora, I pray for you every day."

It's nice she's praying for me, even though I know she doesn't mean for me to think it's nice. I'll bet she doesn't have to pray for Lily and Rose. "Mom, all I'm saying is that if your church is making you miserable, maybe there's one where people, you know, don't irritate you."

Mom shakes her head. We're back at her house and in her driveway, which means the discussion is over because we both know this isn't one we're bringing into the house. "I can't just pull up stakes from my church because someone bugs me, Nora. That's not how it works."

Sitting on her perfect settee, watching a humid Saturday pass me by, I roll her words over in my mind and realize that maybe it's not that easy for her, but it maybe should be. I have my doubts that there's a church out there where a person like me is going to feel at ease, but I keep looking. I'd like to help Mom find a church that gives her more peace than irritation.

My phone buzzes again. Sam, again.

Guess I'll have to worry about my mother's church home another time. I can't ignore Sam forever.

SATURDAY 4:00 PM

I don't have a clue what's going on with Sam. I called her back this morning and got no answer. I sent a text, and still no answer. She's trying to tell me something, and there's a sick feeling in the pit of my stomach that more is going on than just teen angst about moving to a new state.

Jack hasn't returned my message from yesterday either.

Sometimes I envy my parents. They grew up and raised kids in an era when there was one phone in the house and no answering machine. If someone called and you missed it, well, then you missed it. You'd wait until the caller tried again. Now, we have email, social media, text, voice messages, dozens of ways to reach each other and it seems like we're more isolated than we ever were back in the day.

Deep, I know. I sometimes amaze myself with how smart I can be.

I've attempted to write a few pages for the next book, but I haven't been successful. It's not easy for me to write well when I'm trying to hide what I'm doing from my mother, who has an uncanny talent of popping into my room just at the exact moment a great paragraph forms itself in my brain. I realize if she knew what I do for a living, she might be supportive. But the process of getting her to accept that I'm not an invalid, that I don't need a caregiver, and that in fact I'm really quite well off, that would be too much like a confrontation. I don't do confrontation, not in my real life.

Having blown Lily off last night, Mom's going over there for dinner. I'd go, but I don't want to. Lily's cooking makes Rose's health food look like a Roman banquet. Not that I'm a great cook or anything, but Lily is just unimaginative when it comes to food. She's got six recipes in her head and that's what she makes. Saturday night is going to be spaghetti. Mom knows it, I know it, the only one who's surprised is Lily. Given my penchant for making a mess, I avoid dishes like spaghetti when I'm in polite company. For the record, when I'm in polite society, I also avoid corn on the cob, watermelon slices, any kind of soup, and anything that involves blueberry pie filling. I can, and generally will, wind up spilling-wearing-dumping-dropping any one of these foods on myself and others.

So I'm alone in the house and I'm hungry. The chicken from last night is gone. All the leftovers were immediately used for the chicken salad we ate earlier, for a meal my mother called a "little something before dinner." Doesn't matter, it's not like I'm going to waste the energy getting up and dragging myself and my body weight in plaster across the house to the kitchen to find something. Much easier to dial and get someone else to bring me food.

Since Mom lives in a sleepy Waukesha neighborhood, not exactly a vibrant hub of commerce, my options for food delivery are somewhat limited. I look up delivery places on my phone for about fifteen minutes before accepting the fact that I'm getting pizza.

I place my order and arrange myself on the front porch. There's a bit of a breeze this afternoon that's keeping the air from being too sticky and keeping the mosquitoes away. I can't imagine anything worse than a mosquito flying down into my cast. That thing itches as it is.

SATURDAY 5:00 PM

A noise on the porch steps startles me out of a light snooze. I open my eyes and see a guy holding a pizza.

"How much do I owe you?"

"It's already paid for. You were sleeping so I paid the guy."

Of course it would be helpful if I could recognize voices. I study the man in front of me, although I have no idea why. It's not like I'm going to recognize him. I mean, maybe this is how I die. I'm about to be murdered by a guy who just paid for my pizza and waited for me to wake up.

See what kind of fear I live with? No wonder family reunions put me into a froth when I was little. All those furry faced aunts wanting to hug and kiss me. It was stranger danger overload.

Even now, while I'm fairly certain I'm not going to be murdered by this person, I still have a gnawing fear in the pit of my stomach. Normally I go into fight or flight mode, but since flight is pretty much nixed, I just tense up.

"Nora, it's Jack."

I've heard about this in books and movies and stuff, but I guess it actually happens: My heart skips a full beat. He takes a step closer to me and then I see his bright, sparkling blue eyes. My logical brain tells me this isn't a great sign that he just showed up on the porch, but my illogical brain, the part of my brain that functions most of the time because it controls my fight or flight impulses, is doing a little happy dance of joy.

"Wow, Jack."

That's all I can manage. I'm overwhelmed because I thought our friendship was over. I haven't had a lot in the way of friends, I'm not familiar with the concept of making up after a fight. And because everyone around me is so fulfilled in all their perfect human connections, arguments are all but illegal.

"Yeah. I figured I should come down and see you after I got your phone message."

"Is Sam with you?" I look around him to the car parked on the street.

I'm not sure why, but when I look back at Jack, he seems...crestfallen. That's the only word I have for it. Like a deflated balloon.

He sits in the chair next to mine and sets the pizza box on the wicker table between us. For a few minutes we eat silently, filling our faces with pizza to keep from saying anything stupid. Unfortunately, the pizza doesn't last as long as my anxiety.

"So Sam called you?"

Jack's not facing me. He's watching the street like if he stares hard enough it might do a trick.

I've known Jack since high school but when every time you see someone, it's the first time, it takes a moment or two to get into the stream of the unspoken conversation. Jack's got something on his mind, something big enough he drove down here from Manitowoc without Sam.

"She did. She said you were moving to St. Louis."

"The shop's not doing great. My uncle reached out to me last week and asked if I wanted to come work for him and take over his shop when he retires."

"I didn't know you had an uncle."

"My family," he shakes his head. "I guess my mom and her brother got into some fight recently and his way of getting back at her is by talking to me."

Jack's family is polar opposite of mine. Where mine is a giant tribe of people who can finish each other's sentences, Jack's parents haven't spoken to him in years. He thinks it's because Sam was conceived and born out of wedlock. I'm a little more cynical. I'm thinking it's more because keeping Sam meant Jack lost his college scholarship and wound up owning a dying fix it shop in his home town. Either way, if I'm guessing right, the silent treatment spread beyond the immediate family.

For all my family's shortfalls when it comes to my face blindness, at least they still try. They get it wrong most of the time and it's awkward, but at least I know they are trying. There's a comfort in that.

Now, Jack's problem, as I see it, is an easy fix. I could whip out my Pay Pal debit card and just pay whatever outstanding bills he has and make everything awesome for him and for Sam. Then they could stay in Manitowoc and be my friends and help me not freak out when I have to find a missing child.

The thing is, as great as Jack's been about my face blindness, I'm not sure I'm ready to reveal to him what I do for a living. Besides, if I dumped a pile of money on him, it would make him feel lousy about yelling at me in the church parking lot. And it would feel like I'm buying his forgiveness.

I'd be okay with all of that. But I'm new to this friendship thing and I've been told that's not how it's supposed to go.

"You'd sell the shop then, the one in Manitowoc?"

He nods.

"Sam's not on board with the idea of moving. I can tell you that." I doubt I'm giving away any secrets. I'm sure Miss Samantha has made her opinion of the move clear.

He nods again. "She's never lived anywhere but Manitowoc. I haven't either, not really. It's home. And St. Louis is such a huge place, I don't know how great a town it would be to raise a girl."

There's a sharp pain in my head. I know the door at the end of my mind's hallway, the one in the darkest of corners, is rattling, trying to open. I shake it off. "There's no way you can stay?"

"Business hasn't been great for a while, and I'm trying to keep wages for my guys at a livable level, but doing that means I don't pay myself. I've taken loans out against the business and against the house and it hasn't helped. Basically, this is a lifeline to keep us from drowning. I can't see any way out other than taking it."

Now, at this point, someone in my position, someone with enough money to fix everything, would suggest, you know, fixing everything. But it takes me too long to put the words together in my mouth because the next thing Jack says is:

"I'd like it if you moved down there with us."

Of all the things I expected to hear from him, an invitation to move to another state was not one of them. I haven't a clue what my expression was, but I'm guessing it made the thoughts in my head pretty clear to anyone within ten feet of me.

Jack clears his throat and tries again. "What I mean is, you are very important…to Sam. And you told me once you really don't live anywhere, you just stay with your mom when you're not camping on the road. So why not…why not move to St. Louis and live closer to us?"

A far less scandalous offer than one might have assumed. "This would be for Sam's sake?" I'm going to poke the bear good and hard.

He nods. "For Sam's sake. She's getting older and she needs a…"

"Mother figure?"

"Yes, mother figure." He nods again, not realizing the can of worms he's just opened. I'm a little disappointed he's this easy to trap.

"Did you forget what you said to me the last time we talked?"

Can someone blush and turn white at the same time? Because I do believe that's what's happening to Jack's face at this exact moment.

"I haven't forgotten. I just realized…"

Beads of sweat have begun rolling down my leg into my cast. It is not a pleasant sensation. I'm an impatient person as it is, and this conversation is starting to test my very weak limits. "What, you realized you were wrong? You realized I'm not a bad influence on your daughter? You realized I'm not the worst person who ever crossed your path?"

He shakes his head. "No. I mean, yeah, I realized all that. But…also that…also that I really care for you and moving so far away from you…I can't do that. This whole silence thing we've had since Superior…I've been miserable. It's like, I found you again, and then I just ruined everything."

I have lost all feeling in my face. I put my hands on my cheeks just to make sure my skin hasn't somehow melted off and is now lying in a puddle at my feet.

Wait. Wait. Let me back up a bit: Jack just said he cares about me. He. Cares. About. Me.

No man, other than my father, has ever said that to me. I do not date much, and generally nothing past a first date. Much like going to church, I've found that going on a date is an invitation to all sorts of disasters. I decided a decade ago that I wasn't going to inflict that much damage on myself willingly. Hence, the hair, the tattoos, the piercings, all the "stay back" warnings I can muster. Yet here I sit, my high school crush, the only guy I ever really had any kind of feelings for, is telling me he cares about me and wants me to be part of his life.

"I'm not suggesting anything…immoral…if that's what you're worried about." Jack scuffs his foot against the porch slats. "I mean, I'm not asking you to live with me, with us…" he takes a deep breath. "This is a huge step, Nora. I am terrified to make it alone and I am praying you could be a part of it, to help me, to help Sam."

I look at the heavens, wishing that just once, just once, God would open up the sky and just tell me what I'm supposed to do. No poetry, no archaic language, just plain English words that let me know He's not just toying with me for His amusement.

But, as my father always told me, God doesn't work like that these days. God gave us the Bible and pretty much lets us figure it out.

Just my luck. I was born a couple millennia too late. I missed the time when God just looked down and talked to people.

The drops of sweat are seriously causing me discomfort, and I need a break in the intense vibe that's wafting off Jack like some kind of radiation waves. "Look, can we go inside where there's air conditioning?"

"Oh, sure, yes." He hops up and very tenderly helps me through the door into the cool of the house. Given the revelation of his feelings, this is a fresh new experience, this being treated nicely by a guy. I sort of like it.

But not enough to move to St. Louis.

SATURDAY 6:30 PM

"Nora I'm home, it's me, your mother!" Good old Mom, bless her sense of timing, arrives home just as Jack and I are getting me and Mega Cast into a comfortable position on the settee. To say my mother is old-school is an understatement, so my guess is she's not overly joyful when she finds a sweaty Jack standing over a rumpled me. Granted, there is a completely innocent explanation for this, which does not involve nudity in any way, but my mom, good woman that she is, lives in constant fear for her daughter's virtue.

Gotta be honest, my virtue has rarely been threatened.

"Well, Nora. Would you like to introduce me to your friend?"

Nope. Would like everyone to vanish. Would like to go back to the moment when I kicked the piles of boxes and tell myself that kicking said boxes is not going to give me the release I'm looking for. Would like to go back fifteen years and ask my father, who would never lie to me, what on earth Mom meant when she said "we found you."

But introduce Jack? Nope.

"Hello again, Mrs. Hill," Jack stands and extends his hand.

Just my luck. He's got perfect manners.

"I'm Jack Terrell. We spoke on the phone earlier this summer. I was Nora's math tutor in high school."

Oh yes, this is good. Jack and Mom reminiscing about a time when I wasn't at my best. I loathed high school and it felt the same about me. Now here's Jack, who just revealed he'd like to move our relationship into a more romantic realm, chatting like an old friend with my mother, who dreams of the day I'll be settled so she doesn't have to worry I'll set fire to myself or something when it's time for her to go to Heaven.

"Oh yes, Jack. Of course I remember you."

Oh yeah, bring up yet another awesome chapter in the book of Nora…the time I lost my phone and my mother found it.

How about when we talk about a time I wasn't a goofy misfit?

Oh, wait. There is no time like that.

"So Jack, what brings you to Waukesha?"

"Well, Ma'am, I'm here to ask Nora to move to St. Louis with me and my daughter."

Watching my mother's expression melt as she's absorbing this statement is sort of like watching an oil slick roll towards an open flame. You just know it's gonna blow up in spectacular fashion and there's no way you're going to get out of the way in time.

"I'm sorry…I must have misunderstood you. Did you just say you're here to ask my daughter to move in with you?"

Give Brenda some credit. She didn't end the sentence with, "in your group home for mentally deficient wayward losers?" At least she believes I'm capable of stirring some kind of sinful desire in the heart of this guy.

Jack blushes. So endearing.

"No, Mrs. Hill, I didn't explain this right. See, my daughter and I are moving to St. Louis soon. I've got a job offer down there. Nora and I are friends, and she's close to my girl Sam. I figured since Nora doesn't really have…"

He pauses, looking for the right word. I don't blame him. Informing my mother that I don't have a home…that would not be the smart thing to say.

"I wanted to know if Nora would be willing to relocate to St. Louis to live closer to us and help me with Samantha."

Not a great save, but a save nonetheless.

Of course the very idea that anyone would want me to help with a teen aged girl is complete nonsense to my loving mother.

"Mr. Terrell, I don't mean to be rude, but you want Nora to help out with your daughter in some way?"

Jack nods. "Yes, Ma'am. Sam's just turned fourteen and she's gotten to be more of a handful than I know what to do with. Nora's been a great friend to us, I hoped she could give Sam a woman's guidance."

Brenda Hill can't help it. A laugh bursts out of her before she can clamp it down. Jack gives me a shocked look and I shrug. This reaction is nothing surprising to me.

"Mrs. Hill, I'm very sincere. I'm asking Nora for a favor, not for any sort of…immoral reason."

Not quite the feeling I got a few moments ago, but at least Jack understands his audience. Most people would think that protecting the virginity of a thirty-three year old woman is not only silly, it's impossible because how many of us are there in this day and age?

Well, one for sure. And to be otherwise would be the ultimate disappointment to my parents. Frankly, I've given them enough of that in my life. I don't need to pile it on.

"I'm sorry, but I don't understand. How can you think Nora is capable of that kind of responsibility?"

"Ma'am?"

"Mr. Terrell, certainly she's told you about her mental problems. She's not really able to take care of herself. In fact, I've been in touch with her caregiver frequently. I call her every week to check on Nora's progress."

I bite the inside of my mouth to keep from howling with laughter. If by 'caregiver' she means Connie, and I'm sure she does, I can only imagine the rage my agent flies into every time Mom calls. It's a good thing I'm talented and my books sell ridiculously well.

I should probably send Connie some pages.

And maybe a gift basket of muffins or something.

Of course, if she's on one of her made-up diets, like the one where she could eat anything she wanted to as long as she chewed bubble gum while she was eating, then she won't be my biggest fan for sending her food.

Do they make celery gift baskets?

"Mrs. Hill, I appreciate your concern for Nora, but she's an adult."

Good luck convincing Brenda of that fact Jack.

I glance at Mom and shockingly she's not loading up a retort to Jack's challenge. She's staring at me like she used to when we were in church and I wasn't paying close enough attention. It's that look moms have when they want to yell at their kids, but they are in a place where yelling is just not going to be acceptable. If I'm measuring my mother's desire to yell at me by the intensity of her glare, I'm guessing the walls would be rattling at this point if Jack wasn't sitting here.

The phone rings and breaks the spell. Mom goes to the kitchen to answer the phone. Why did she have to go to another room?

Let me explain my mother and her relationship with technology.

Brenda Hill is very good at many things. She is the person you want in your corner if you need volunteers to collect food, gather baby blankets, or serve a meal. She can organize a funeral dinner in her sleep. She can lead an army of women across the city for all manner of charitable reasons without breaking a sweat. There is no church need to big for Brenda Hill.

However…

She prefers to run a less than mobile command post. More to the point, she prefers that all incoming calls come to her fifty-year-old rotary phone, which is attached to her kitchen wall. Oh she knows how to use a cell phone. She has a cell phone she uses liberally, but only with the family. She could get rid of that olive green beast in ten seconds and the world would rejoice, but she refuses to. She is convinced that any and all church business, and thusly any and all Brenda Hill business, must be conducted on a "safe" phone line. And cell phones, she has told us time and time again, are not safe.

"They are easily stolen or lost," is her mantra. "No one has ever lost or stolen my kitchen phone."

My sisters were fairly grumbly to me when I managed to prove Mom's point by losing my cell phone in her garage. Now she does deign to take calls on the cell, but only from family. Which is why it shocks me that she called my contacts when she found my phone.

Anyway, her phone rings and she gets up to get it. I'm sitting there, staring at Jack, trying to sort out what he said to me on the porch. The idea that he might have some sort of feeling for me doesn't exactly make me uncomfortable, which is weird. But Jack's only slightly better at expressing himself than I am, so I'm not running out to buy the white dress just yet.

"Nora, that was the strangest call."

I blink at Mom. Tiny tendrils of pain are starting to spread throughout my brain. I look at Jack, who is staring back at me, and not wearing a nervous smile anymore. "Who was that?"

"That was Janet Keen." Mom's face looks like a mask stretched too tightly.

"Who is Janet Keen?" Jack looks at me and I shrug. The name's not ringing any bells.

Mom returns to her seat at the table. "Janet Keen is Cassie Wilson's mother. She called to see if I thought Cassie looked okay at the funeral."

The first ghostly fingers of a headache wrap themselves around my head. I don't like where this is going.

"She said Cassie's seemed strange ever since she found out she was pregnant."

"Strange, how?" My voice sounds very far away.

Mom sits and folds her hands in front of her, a sure sign that she's concerned about something. "Strange, like she's hiding something from Janet."

"Well, Cassie's a married adult. I don't imagine she tells her mother everything all time. That's sort of Casper's job." Look at me, trying to be logical.

"Yes, well, unlike some daughters I know, Cassie still loves her mother does, in fact, tell Janet everything."

And look at Mom, firing back with a heaping helping of mom guilt.

"Cassie's husband's name is Casper, like the ghost?"

70

We both look at Jack. I think Mom and I both forgot he was there.

"Janet said she and Cassie went grocery shopping today and Cassie seemed to be hiding something. Also, she thought Cassie might have fallen or somehow injured herself because she was moving as if she was in pain."

Why this is happening, I can't say, but now I know what's going on with me. There's no denying it. It feels like shards of glass are being driven into my skull. I take a deep breath, hoping I can stave off the inevitable. "Jack!" I reach my hands out toward him. I'm vaguely aware that Jack catches me as I slide out of my chair and into darkness.

SATURDAY 7:30 PM

I open my eyes to the dulcet tones of my mother's "yelling but not yelling" voice. I don't know how long I've been out, but I know it's been long enough for Jack to get into an ultra-polite, super tense, discussion about whether or not to call an ambulance. Bonus, I'm hearing two extra voices which can only mean one thing: My sisters are here.

I'm lying on the thickly padded Oriental rug that covers eighty percent of the dining room floor. Mom and Jack are kneeling beside me. My hearing isn't perfect, of course, but my guess is that my sisters are in the front room, as if that short distance somehow keeps them from becoming actively involved in the discussion.

"She doesn't need to go to the ER, Mrs. Hill. She's done this before."

"I'm aware that she's done this before, Mr. Terrell. She did it yesterday at the deli."

"She did this before?" One of my sisters barks. "Why are we even asking the question then? Clearly something's wrong with her."

"Yes, clearly something's wrong with her." Another sister echoes.

Okay, now I know who's who. Lily, the older sister, is the imperious one and Rose is the parrot. They are almost physically identical, so much so that they often passed for twins in school, even though there's a year between them in age. Rose defers to Lily for almost everything which actually makes it easier for me to tell them apart when we're together.

No one's noticed I'm back in the land of the conscious, and I'm not about to interrupt the debate going on over my prone body. It's rather entertaining, listening to people talk about you when they think you can't hear them.

"Nothing is wrong with her. It's her…thing." Jack, on my right, gives my hand a light squeeze. I'm not sure if he's trying to wake me up or give me reassurance. Since I haven't opened my eyes, my guess is it's the former, so I can prove I'm not in the middle of some dire health emergency.

"Prosopagnosia is not her 'thing' Mr. Terrell. It's a mental illness."

I would love to yell, but I keep my thought to myself. Actually, Mom, it's a neurological disorder, but that's not the thing Jack's talking about.

I know why Jack's not offering information immediately. He knows I'm not comfortable with my ability to track down missing kids. Most people would think of it as a gift, but not me. It's just too weird, the way I know I have to find someone and then it's weirder, the way I actually do it. Jack's the only person on earth who knows that I wrestle with this because if I admitted my reluctance to anyone else, I'd come off as some kind of child- hating monster.

Jack squeezes my hand again and this time I look up and right into those lovely blue eyes of his. He gives me a half smile and whispers, "Welcome back." He helps me slowly, gently, up to a sitting position. This goes unnoticed by my female relatives, because they are deeply engrossed in discussing whether or not face blindness is a mental illness. It's an old argument and I haven't a clue why the three of them feel the need to rehash it since they agree with each other.

Sometimes I think they argue because they've run out of things to talk about and arguing gives them a reason to stay in contact. If they didn't all live in each other's back yards this would not be a problem.

I live in my car most of the time, you'd think they'd love to hear what I have to say.

"Would you three keep it down please?"

I'm pretty sure Jesus Himself couldn't have shocked my female relatives into such a complete silence.

"Now, all three of you, please sit on the couch." I nod to Jack who helps me and my cast into a chair. "I'm going to explain something and you're going to listen to me and not interrupt." I hold up a hand, stopping Lily from what I know will be the first of many interruptions.

With Jack sitting next to me I have the courage...okay I have the weakest of resolve...in telling them about finding missing children. I may not recognize faces, but I know expressions well enough to realize that this little talent of mine is shocking to them. I try not to let that stop me from getting to the point that's most pressing on my mind. "So the question is, why would I need to look for Cassie Wilson?"

"Good question, since she's an adult who isn't even missing," Lily mutters.

"She's a member of our church," Rose points out a bit louder. "Helping her would be the right thing to do."

"That has nothing to do with it." I can't keep a heavy sigh from escaping. "Up until now it's only been kids, under the age of fifteen or sixteen. I've never had to look for an adult or a family or anything like that."

"So these blackouts have nothing to do with your health?" Lily is clearly disappointed that Mom dragged her from her Saturday evening Bible Yoga class (it's a thing, believe it out not.) All the willowy perfect moms get together, do yoga, and recite Bible passages at each other.

Sounds really, really terrible, if you ask me. No offense to anyone, but that just sounds like the Bible is being forced onto something just so the women involved can feel like they're doing something for the church. But who am I to judge?

"No, Lily, it has nothing to do with my health."

"You recognized me?" Lily seems shocked. So do Rose and Mom. They all turn and stare at me like I'm a circus animal who's just done a spectacular trick.

I can't even get upset by this, since, truth be told, I don't talk about face blindness much with my family. They think I'm mentally deficient and I really haven't done much to persuade them otherwise. But, since all the pieces of my nicely cubby holed life have just crashed into each other, I suppose now is a good time to explain it all. "It doesn't work like that. You've been sitting there and you haven't moved for a while. If you left the room and came back five minutes later, in a different outfit, I wouldn't recognize you."

Lily and Rose nod sagely, as if this is knowledge they had and they are proud of me for explaining it so clearly. My mother looks befuddled.

"So, Nora, all this time, you've recognized us?"

"Once I figure out who everyone is, yes. As long as you don't change your clothes or leave my sight for more than five, maybe ten minutes."

"It helps if you just tell her your name when you walk up to her," Jack adds.

"Yes, thank you for that, Mr. Terrell." My mother gives him a warning look, like she's not at all overjoyed that he, a stranger, understands my issues better than she does.

"Let's get back to Cassie," Rose redirects the energy in the room. "So why is it you think you have to find her?"

"Well, I don't have to find her because she's not missing...yet." I try not to sound too sarcastic. "So I'm

confused why I'm getting the headache and the black out for
an adult who isn't missing, just maybe not telling her
mother the whole truth about something."

"So what, do you have to go touch her coat or
something? Get her scent?" Lily asks.

I can't help it. "I'm not a bloodhound, Lil."

"I didn't mean…"

"I know, I know." I hold up my hand to stave off
further sisterly bickering. "Sometimes I do look at an item
the missing child owns, but it doesn't really help all that
much. Mostly I have to wait."

"For what, dear?"

I look at my mother. Again, I can't resist the
temptation. "For the voice of God," I reply in my most
dramatic tone.

"Or a vision." Jack adds helpfully.

"Right. A voice or a vision. I have to wait for one or
the other."

"That doesn't sound very…real." Rose is a sort of
Doubting Thomas sometimes. She has full faith in God. She
doesn't question a single word in the Bible. But anything
else that might touch on the mystical, that she has to see to
believe.

"It does sound rather, loosey goosey, Nora," Mom
says.

So, Moses and Elijah and Elisha, they can all do miracles and hear God's voice right in their heads, and that's fine. But little old me…I'm being loosey goosey.

Jack comes to my rescue. "That's what I thought at first until I saw her in action."

The shock on their faces is about as dramatic as if Jack had told them we'd eloped and were now going to live on an island in the South Pacific and raise miniature donkeys. But I give Jack credit. He doesn't wimp out.

"I've seen her track down two children this summer. Kids that would have died if she hadn't found them." Jack gives me a smile that makes my stomach flutter a little. It's a weird sensation for me.

"Nora…is this true?"

I only nod at Mom, still trying to shake the fluttery feeling, and hoping I don't have some stupid look on my face.

"Is your caregiver aware that you're able to do this?"

The question snaps me back into reality. Jack's expression has melted into confusion and my sisters are now nodding at my mother as if this very thought had crossed their minds.

"Caregiver?" Jack whispers.

"Connie."

"Who's Connie?"

"My agent."

"You have an agent?" Jack probes.

Oh brother. In all this tangle I'd forgotten that the one thing no one knows is how I support myself. The last piece of my life's puzzle hovers over Jack and me. Not really. I mean, there isn't actually a puzzle piece hanging over us. Although that would be entertaining. "I'll explain later. Just go with it."

He doesn't look convinced, but I think he'll play along.

"Look, Mom, Connie is not a caregiver. She's sort of a…friend. And you have to stop calling her. She's a busy person."

"She's never too busy to talk to me."

I'll bet. I can just imagine Connie happily taking my mother's calls, hoping against hope Brenda will spill some deep dark secret Connie can use to force me to do a book signing. "Whatever. Can we get back to Cassie Wilson? That's the real issue here. There's a good chance that if something hasn't happened to her yet, it may."

"Would you like me to call her mother back and find out?"

I'm always amazed that the solution to every problem in Brenda Hill's world is to call someone's mother. I've noticed my sisters have started to do this too. Is there some secret network of mothers where one phone call will solve a problem? Because in my experience, calling my mother has only created more chaos. But maybe it's different if she's the one doing the calling. I don't know. I've never been a mother so I don't have the membership card.

"Maybe I could talk to her husband." I say this just to ease the expectant looks on everyone's face. Clearly, they still think this is some kind of magic act and I'm going to pull Cassie out of my coat pocket and everything will be fine.

"I could call Casper. I've got his number right here." Rose holds up her phone.

My mother gives her a withering look. "Why would you have Casper Wilson's phone number? And why would he answer your call if he isn't answering Janet's?"

Bigger question...why would anyone name their son Casper? And then why would he marry someone named Cassandra?

"Mom, it's not the 1950's. Casper is a friend of mine. We did that food drive at church together, remember?" Rose sighs. "And maybe Mrs. Keen is being a little nosy and he doesn't feel like talking to his mother-in-law at this second."

I'm not sure who's more shocked right now: Brenda, because Rose has a man's phone number and doesn't think this is a gateway to adultery, or me because Rose has really gotten sassy lately. I'm a little peeved. Sassy is my thing.

While they're barking at each other about how proper it is to have someone's phone number, Jack leans closer to me. "Is talking to this guy going to help?"

I shake my head and grin. "Probably not, but it gives them something to discuss."

"I'm starting to see why you live in your car."

Best words anyone's ever said to me. I mean, Jack's starting to get it. Living with my mother, with my sisters so close, is sort of like being in a church Ladies' Aid group that never, ever ends. God bless them, they mean well, but ultimately many of their discussions and debates are over nothing that's going to change the course of history. I sat in on a Ladies' Aid meeting once when Rose first joined and asked that I come along. They were trying to decide which picture of the church they should use for the connect cards and visitor thank you notes. Seriously, the debate raged for over an hour and had to be tabled to the next meeting because the youth group needed the fellowship hall for a cooking demonstration. That was something like ten years ago. From what I hear, they still haven't decided on which picture to use. The sole point of dispute is the shading of the pew cushions. In one photo they look bright red. In another, slightly less bright red. The fine ladies of the church are evenly split over this. My mother was president at the time they started. She retired ten years later and to this day she has regrets she wasn't able to settle the issue. It's still not settled. I can't make this stuff up.

My two brothers-in-law are wonderful, long-suffering guys who work on cars in their garages...a lot. I don't have a garage, so I disappear for weeks on end and live in my car. And Jack's finally understanding why.

It's a nice feeling.

I shake my head free of this new, unexpected sensation of happiness. I have to focus on the bickering that's happening because unless I get everyone on the same page, or at least in the same hymnal, I'm never going to get out of my mother's dining room. I'm never going to find Cassie Wilson, and then it's St. Louis all over again.

St. Louis. Jack is moving there.

If he moves there.

I'll never see him again because I promised myself I would never go back to that town. Deep, deep down at the end of the hallway of locked doors in my brain is the door with the heaviest locks, and that's St. Louis. It was the one time I didn't get there in time and the kid died. I promised I would never go back to that town, or to that feeling. I look at Jack and suddenly my stomach twists and my head is pounding. I really need to stop toying with the past and focus on the task at hand.

"Mom…Mom! Rose! Lily!" I hold up a hand and wave at them, hoping to silence the din of their squawking. "I need to have some quiet to focus on this."

"Oh, of course. Hey, I have an idea. We'll go sit out on the porch in the scorching heat and wait for you to hear your little voice or get your vision and then we'll all pack into the car and go get Cassie." Lily crosses her arms, having made up her mind that my talent, my gift, whatever, is fake and I'm just her dumb little sister. "Of course, I'm not sure there's a real talent to finding someone who isn't actually missing."

"Lily, don't be mean." Rose has always been slightly kinder to me. "Nora can't help the way she is, we've always known that. Just let her think she can find Cassie. What could it hurt?"

I did say she was the slightly kinder sister. Emphasis on the word "slightly."

"Girls, if Nora says she's able to find Cassie if and when she goes missing, I say we need to believe her."

It's the biggest ringing endorsement I've ever gotten from my mother. I hate to shred this slender tendril of support, but I've got this obstinate streak and I can't help it. "To be accurate, I didn't say I would find her. I said I'm supposed to find her. Or rather, I'm supposed to find her before something really horrible happens to her."

"What like you've been chosen?" Lily glares at me.

"Something like that."

Rose taps her Fit Bit. Or course she has a Fit Bit, both my sisters do. They call each other every day to make sure they're meeting or exceeding their step goals. It's not like either one of them has to watch their weight all the closely. I mean, I don't think about what I eat or how much I exercise and I weigh less than most twelve year olds. But they are former pageant winners who also happen to subscribe to the whole, "your body is a temple" ideal.

Anyway, where was I? Right, so Lily also looks at the time on her Fit Bit and shakes her head. "Look, I've got to get the kids ready for bed. Church is tomorrow." She stands. "Let me know when this whole cry for attention ends."

Jack is looking at me, his blue eyes pleading with me to defend myself. For whatever reason, Jack Terrell, the guy who yelled at me about being a bad influence on his daughter, believes in me in this moment and wants me to stand up for myself.

Me standing up for myself has never been part of the family dynamic. My sisters have always believed I do things to get attention when the opposite is true. Every tattoo, every hair color, every trip away from home has been a cry to be left alone. But they see it otherwise and I guess Lily

82

has had enough. She walks to the door and I am going to let her.

Except…

"I'm not crying for attention. This is what I do, Lily. I find missing children who are at risk of dying."

I have no idea where those words came from. Better yet, I have no idea where the courage for those words came from.

"I'm sure you believe that." She looks even less convinced as she opens the door, letting the steamy air in. "But I have real things to do."

Lily steps out into the dying day's sunlight and Rose gets up. Her expression is a weak imitation of Lily's but still not one that offers any sisterly support to me. "I'm sorry, Nora, it's just a bit much, you know, coming from you."

She leaves and the door closes behind her. All that's left of my sisters is a heavy breath of humid air, and the AC wipes that out in a minute.

My mother watches the door as if waiting for the girls to return. After almost a full minute, she sighs heavily and stands. "I suppose I'm going to go to bed."

I'm sure I'm wearing the same surprised look on my face as Jack is. "Mom, it's not even eight-thirty. You don't have to go to bed."

My mother smiles softly. She looks almost…angelic. It's weird. "Nora, you and Mr. Terrell have some things to talk about. And I don't want to get in the way of whatever it is you're going to do for Cassie Wilson. You just go ahead and work on that. Service is at eight tomorrow, remember. Mr. Terrell, will you be joining us for church?"

Jack shakes his head. "No ma'am. I have to drive back up to Manitowoc tonight yet. I told my daughter I'd be home tonight."

"Well I hope you bring her down next time." Mother waves at us as if she's standing on the deck of some luxury liner, bidding us farewell before she leaves on her voyage.

Once we're alone I look at Jack and start laughing. I can't help it. My family seems utterly normal to me until I think about what an outsider might be seeing. "They are fun, aren't they?"

Jack shakes his head. "Meeting your family definitely puts some pieces of the puzzle into place."

We are silent for a moment and I realize I don't want him to leave just yet. "Do you have to go right away?"

"I should. Sam's actually staying with Mary Jo and her family while I'm down here."

Mary Jo Pelnar is a mother of several children and a woman who was my friend during my horrible high school years. She's a strong Catholic with a sharp tongue and a huge heart and if I had to pick one person who is my very best friend, I would say it's her. "I didn't know you and Mary Jo were friends."

"We aren't, really. But she brought her car and half her children into the shop one day after you'd been up there and we got to talking. Her oldest and Sam are about the same age. I guess the girls hit it off. She's been a godsend for us, a real mother figure." Jack keeps his eyes firmly glued to Brenda Hill's beloved lace table cloth, but the irony of his words is not lost on me. "It's going to be hard to move away from her."

This is why I work very hard to avoid creating bonds with people. It just complicates things. "So if I moved down there, I'd be what, a fill in for Mary Jo?"

Jack snaps out of his study of the table cloth and looks at me, his cheeks pinking up with a mixture of embarrassment and possibly anger. "No, nothing like that. I told you why I want you to move to St. Louis."

He did. To be fair, he did. But there's a perverse spot in my heart that wants to hear certain words. I don't even know what those words are, but I know I'll recognize them if he speaks them. "Fine. Okay. Let's not fight."

"Can we get out of here? Maybe take a walk...oh, wait." He glances at my cast. "Sorry."

"Don't be. We can drive downtown. I mean, we won't be able to walk along the river, but it'll be a change of scenery from this."

"Your car or mine?"

"Let's take mine...there's more leg room."

I lean on him heavily as we make our way out of my mother's house and to my Forester.

SATURDAY 9:00 PM

So no, we can't walk around Frame Park. Instead, we're sitting on a metal bench outside Divino Gelato,

85

indulging in the icy cold Italian treats that particular eatery has to offer. I'm working my way through a small bowl of sour cherry, while Jack is digging deep into a large mixture of dark chocolate and peanut butter. On a Saturday night the Civic Theater acts as an anchor for all the restaurants and art shops in the Historic Downtown area. Later things will get a bit more rowdy when the Art Crawl turns into a Pub Crawl, but for now it's a family friendly, lively atmosphere, just right for two people who are trying to avoid talking about something important.

"Nora? Nora Hill? Is that you?"

A woman walks up to us. This is my worst moment. Clearly this is a person who knows me, but obviously I haven't a clue who she is. I tense.

"It is you, Nora, your mother didn't tell me you were in town."

So…this is a person who knows my mother. That narrows it down to about half of Waukesha County.

"Yeah. I am. I'm…sort of stuck here." I point to my cast.

"Oh you poor thing." The woman makes that clucking noise older women make when they mean to sound sympathetic.

"Hello ma'am, I'm Jack, a friend of Nora's." Jack stands and holds out his hand.

"Oh, hello. I'm Kimmy Wilson, Casper Wilson's mother. We know Nora's family from church."

Jack has in one move helped me and made my life more difficult. Casper Wilson's mother would be Cassie Wilson's mother-in-law. My head starts to throb again and little pin points of light blur my vision. I blink. I am so not fainting in front of this woman.

"So how's Cassie these days?" Why I bring up the very point I'd like to avoid is beyond me.

Mrs. Wilson's smile melts away. "Well she's just fine, I suppose. She's pregnant and it's summer, so I'm sure she's a bit uncomfortable but she's fine otherwise. Now that she and Casper have ironed out their…difficulty."

My senses tingle. "Their difficulty?"

Mrs. Wilson waves her hand. "Oh you know young couples when they're expecting that first child."

No. I don't. But my head is throbbing even more.

I glance at Jack who is frowning. He shakes his head slightly, and I know we are in agreement. If Mrs. Wilson isn't going to bring it up, I'm not going to.

I must be staring at her, because Mrs. Wilson clears her throat in that uncomfortable way old ladies do. "Well, dear, it's been nice seeing you, but I must go. We'll see you in church." Mrs. Wilson waves as she rejoins her group, a gaggle of older women all wearing brightly colored polyester pull up pants and coordinating sweater sets.

If I ever get too old to put on blue jeans, someone is just going to have to put me in a room and hide me. I may be riddled with issues, but I have some standards and one of them is I'm never going to stoop to wearing polyester pull up pants. Never.

"So that's the woman that named her kid after a cartoon ghost." Jack returns his attention to his gelato.

"Yeah." I rub my head, a move Jack doesn't miss.

"Are you getting something?"

I blink and try to concentrate, but there's nothing. I don't see anything, I don't hear anything. I know I'm supposed to find Cassie, at least I think I am, but I still don't know why.

"Her comments about young couples felt weird, but I don't know. Maybe Mrs. Keen is just fretting about nothing, like my sisters think." I know I'm saying this to alleviate my growing sense of dread. And it doesn't work.

"Maybe." Jack draws the word out, voicing his doubts in two syllables.

I take another mouthful of gelato when a lightning bolt strikes my brain. Some would brush it off and say I have an ice cream head ache, but I know better. This is a summons, and no mistaking it. I close my eyes and wait.

I don't want to keep my eyes closed too long, or I'll forget what Jack looks like sitting on the bench next to me. That used to happen when I was little and didn't understand face blindness. I would be sitting next to my sister in church and I'd close my eyes for a couple minutes (because let's be honest, most of the time sitting still during sermons is a sleep tonic to little kids. Even when I thought my father was the voice of the Almighty, I couldn't always keep my eyes open.) Anyway, when I opened my eyes again, there would be two strangers on either side of me. I would freak out, and of course Mother would punish me when we got home. My defense was my sisters were playing a mean trick on me, but of course that sounded like nonsense because no one moved from their seats.

It's probably one of the bigger reasons I haven't been able to find a church where I'm comfortable. Too many bad flashbacks of "go to church, get punished after."

I open my eyes, the lightning bolt having eased, and Jack is studying me intently.

"No, I don't know anything specific." I shake my head. "But I feel like there's water involved."

Jack sits back against the bench and sighs. "That's what happened last time, in Superior."

"True, but then I knew that boy was near water. This time, I just feel like water's...involved. Like Cassie's not in water, or on water. But..."

"Maybe she's drinking water?"

I know Jack's trying to be funny. I get it. I'm just super frustrated about this. I mean, my whole "finding kids" thing is weird enough. Not exactly a calling I'm thrilled to have. But this time everything seems really sketchy, hazy. Almost like something is clouding the process, getting in the way. Like when you tune a radio and you hear bits from two different stations.

I would like to ponder this more, but I'm exhausted. Besides, Jack's got to drive back to Manitowoc. We don't say much as he drives me back to Mom's. He helps me into the house and gets me settled in my makeshift room.

"I don't have to leave tonight, you know. I could stick around another day." Jack drapes a light blanket across me. "It's not like I have a job to go back to. And I'm sure Mary Jo would be fine keeping Sam another day." He shrugs. "I rented a room at The Clark Hotel downtown. Just in case."

"In case of what?" I'm more than a little shocked at the inference of this statement. In case I said yes to his weird non-proposal and we decided to consummate it? Yeah, that wouldn't happen. Even if I weren't completely socially paralyzed, my mother would find out and hell would be a cool dry breeze compared to her wrath in that situation.

Oh, also, I'm insulted that he would even think I'd be that easy.

Right. That's the correct response to him renting a hotel room. We'll go with that. I'm insulted.

"You were making a large assumption."

The minute the words fall out of my mouth I realize I've read the whole thing wrong. I know this mostly because of the next thing Jack does.

He stands up, walks to the door, and turns his back on me. "After everything you know about me, that's where you go when I tell you I got a room? Really?" He faces away from me and I realize this is on purpose. He knows it doesn't take long for me to forget his face.

I didn't realize he could fight dirty.

"Look, Jack…you said you got a room 'just in case.' And you started this little visit by asking me to move to St. Louis with you. So, in case of what? In case I said yes, and that made us a couple that did things like share a hotel room?"

He turns around. Thankfully I still recognize him and his lovely blue eyes. "No, Nora. Of course not. I got a room just a case your life got complicated while I was here and you needed some help with something."

And now I feel horrible. Of course he has nothing but the best intentions. He's not the one wrestling with God about everything. He's standing in the doorway, the dim hall light glowing around him.

Like a stinking halo.

I would literally not even feel worse.

He shakes his head. "I should go. We've got church early in the morning."

"Jack, I'm sorry. I didn't mean to make everything dramatic. If you want to just go back tonight, I would totally understand."

"No, it's fine." He smiles, his lovely eyes twinkling, and I know I'm forgiven. "You're the one who should be worried about tomorrow. You're the one who has drama every time you go to church."

"Yes, but maybe not this time. Hope springs eternal, you know."

He walks back to me and pats my shoulder lightly. There's a heartbeat of awkwardness between us, like there's something he'd like to say…or do yet…but then he heads for the door. "I'll be by at 7:30 to pick you up."

"I'll be here. Probably in this very spot."

I watch him leave before I close my eyes, and try to clear up the fuzzy, indecipherable images running through my brain.

SUNDAY 8:00 AM

On a scale of one to ten, with ten being the most uncomfortable, I give going to church with my entire tribe AND Jack an eleven.

First of all, my sisters are grown women with husbands and children of their own. Why in the world do we all have to squeeze together in one pew every Sunday? But every Sunday, first service, nothing stops the Hills from filling the sixth pew on the right. It's pretty much the longest pew in the building. When I'm not around it's uncomfortable, but today, with Jack and me added, the pew is beyond tight.

I'm on the end, with the arm of the pew digging into my side. Since there's no room for my crutches, those are neatly tucked behind the door in the mothers' room. Which means even if I could get myself out of this tight spot, I wouldn't be able to make a quick escape. But at least I'm not Jack. Poor Jack, he's flattened between Rose and me, and Rose way over-did it with her perfume this morning. Jack's not only a physical buffer between me and my family, he's also a scent sponge, absorbing Rose's cloud of smell before it hits me.

Church should really not be a contact sport.

I'll be honest, I'm not focused on the service one bit. The good news is no one really notices. Everyone, and I do mean everyone, is too busy staring at me, freak show that I am. And then if they dare pull their gaze from me, they're studying Jack up and down, wondering, I'm sure, how such a normal looking guy is a guest of mine. My nieces and nephews are poking each other and pointing and giggling…or they would be if they weren't wedged together so tightly. They remind me of the time Kevin tried to cram a hundred mini marshmallows into his mouth. Spoiler alert: He failed. He gagged so hard around number seventy that he threw up a gummy wad of nicely scented vanilla vomit.

Most important, I'm still trying to sort out the whole Cassie Wilson thing. The last time I found someone I had a very clear vision of water. This time, I sense water is involved, but I don't know how. Nothing is clear. It's still that sort of weird AM radio reception. There are sounds overlapping other sides in my head.

There's a lot of standing and sitting in our service, which is good because it's the only time our sardine pew can breathe. The minister says, "Please rise," and the Hills plus one stand up as a unit and take one giant breath in and out. If I weren't part of this choreography I'd have to excuse myself, go to the mother's room, and muffle my laughter in a nursing chair pillow.

The minister gives the final blessing and the organist crashes into some loud exit music she feels is jazzy enough to get the parishioners out into the mission field with a song in their hearts. I may not recognize faces, but sometimes I recognize expressions and from the looks of it, all she's managed to do is stir some folks out of their sermon induced slumber.

My mother joined this church when she and I moved to Waukesha after my father's death. She picked this church because this is where Rose landed after she got married. Lily went here while she was at Carroll University, and then joined when she married one of the deacons from the congregation. So I'm familiar with the various organists who play here. I'm glad it's the lady who eases us into the service with solemn, worshipful preservice music and then blasts us out the door with the recessional. There's another organist who insists using some sort of chime thingy with every hymn. Those chimes makes the whole service feel like one of those old kids books, the ones that had the records and you read along with the record and turned the page when Tinkerbell twiddled her wand.

Church should not remind people of Tinkerbell. I'm just sayin'.

As I watch the assembly gets ushered out of their pews, I'm pretty proud of myself for getting through a service without any sort of comical disaster befalling me. As we are walking out of our pew, I lay eyes on a very pregnant woman and the thing Kimmy Wilson said about young couples and first babies comes back to me. I feel dizzy. Jack steadies my arm and half drags, half shoves me toward the exit. I must be moving on my own feet at least a little because no one in our camper van of a pew seems to make comment of my departure.

Jack navigates me to the mothers' room, which is blessedly empty. He sits me down in a cushioned rocking chair and kneels in front of me. "What is it? What did you see?"

"Did you see that woman who walked out in front of us?"

Jack nods. "The one in the flowered dress, right? The really pregnant one?"

"That's the one."

94

"That must be Cassie. Since one of the women with her was that lady we saw last night."

I envy his ability to know who people are by looking at them.

I close my eyes. I feel nauseous from the room spinning around me. An upset stomach is sometimes a part of my process so I'm not REALLY worried about that. However, I'm not too keen on blowing out chunks of the oat bran Mom insisted I inhale before church because... you know...being regular is important.

None of it, though, not the nausea, not the Oat Bran, not the crowded church, means anything at this moment. See, a big piece, a massive chuck, of the puzzle has been solved. Of course it just raises more questions, but at least I know now why Cassie Wilson is triggering all my senses.

See, I'm not supposed to keep Cassie Wilson from disaster.

I'm supposed to rescue the baby she's carrying.

SUNDAY 10:00 AM

I don't know how Jack did it and I'm not sure I want to ask, but he got me out of the Hill Family Brunch that happens every Sunday over at Lily's house. Attendance has never been, to this point, voluntary. If you are in town and you are not on your deathbed, you make your way from church to Lily's, and you better be bringing some kind of brunch type dish to pass with you. It's the Hill version of an Easter breakfast pot luck, but it's every week and it's always at Lily's which would be fine except that woman does like to redecorate on a regular basis. This is a problem for me. When we are at my mother's I typically wait until everyone sits because everyone sits in the same chairs they've been sitting in for the last fifteen years. Rose is the same as Mom. I can go to her place and pretty much know who is who by where they are sitting. But Lily changes her furniture a lot. I know her husband is a good man and makes a good living for them, but I've also heard dear old Brenda come down on her eldest daughter about the sin of prideful decorating.

But I needn't fear calling someone by the wrong name today because I have Jack take us to the easily maneuverable brunch at his hotel. The Clark Hotel and Restaurant is one of those historic buildings that's changed hands over the generations and now is doing well as a hotel and Irish pub. The food is good, the pub is popular, and the restaurant itself is peaceful even when it's full. I credit that to the management team, especially the newest member, a culinary student and fellow tattoo enthusiast, Holly. The girl puts her skills to use all over the business, from working the front desk of the hotel to mixing beverages in the pub and baking much of the bread and pastries she serves in the restaurant.

"She looks like she's following in your fashion footsteps," Jack comments as he watches Holly take our order to the kitchen.

"She's got some catching up to do in the tattoo department." I joke, but I know Jack's not wrong. Maybe ten years separate us, but I can tell she's a person searching for the right spiritual home just like I am, and questioning pretty much everything else along the way. I like her. And not just because she makes the best cupcakes I've ever had.

"So what's the deal. Now you're supposed to find a child that's not even born?" Jack takes a sip of coffee. His eyes twinkle over the rim of the cup.

"I guess. I just don't know if it's mother or child that's in trouble."

"Does it matter? Aren't they one and the same at the moment?"

I stare at my coffee, barely hearing Jack's question. In my head there's a whole parade of fuzzy noises. This is different from the still, quiet voice I generally hear when I'm looking for a missing kid. This time it's garbled, like it's layered over another voice.

Weird.

Holly brings us our meals, and Jack and I start eating in silence. Well, Jack's silent. I'm still mentally trying to converse with two mystical voices…or one voice saying two different things at the same time. I'm really not sure.

Anyone who doesn't believe in God has never been in my head. My brain is clearly fearfully and wonderfully made. Emphasis on the fearfully part.

"Is your food okay?" Jack looks up from the mountain of corned beef hash and eggs he's working on.

"Oh yeah, no it's fine." I poke at my Irish Eggs Benedict. What makes them Irish? Probably the slab of Irish cheddar between the ham and the eggs…and the massive pile of oven roasted red potatoes. "I'm just…I'm not getting a clear signal."

"This is a strange one. I mean, have you ever had to find an adult or an unborn child before?"

"Not that I can remember." I shake my head to quiet the stomping in my brain. I know those footsteps, they're headed to the door marked "St. Louis." Seriously, I know I didn't find a child in time in that city…but I remember little else. While I could recite chapter and verse of every other kid I've located, that one eludes me. Probably because I buried it good and solid. That door's not opening. So I silence the footsteps in the hallway of my mind and I focus on the food and on Jack. "What's bugging me is what Mrs. Wilson said."

"Which thing?"

"The thing about young couples and first pregnancies. I mean, what does that mean? When my sisters were pregnant with their first kids it was like Easter and Christmas rolled into one. But Kimmy Wilson sounded like it wasn't that way with Cassie and Casper."

"Those names slay me." Jack grins.

I nod. "Yeah, I know." I poke at my food. "So Cassie's mom thinks there's something wrong with Cassie, like physically. And Casper's mom is chalking up any discord to them being a pregnant couple."

"Right."

"Janet Keen thinks Cassie is hiding something from her. This isn't a big deal to me, I don't come close to telling my mom everything. But Cassie's not like me."

"Nora, no one's like you."

The comment, and the smile that comes along with it, confuse me. Is Jack trying to flirt with me?

This day just gets more and more strange.

"Maybe Cassie did fall or something. I read someplace that pregnant women are clumsy." Jack sips his coffee, as if the whole flirty comment didn't happen.

"Oh that's the truth. Lily tripped a lot. She said it felt like the whole house tilted when she walked. They had her tested for an inner ear thing."

Jack sips his coffee. "So maybe this is all nothing. Cassie's clumsy because she's expecting. She tripped, maybe bruised a hip so she looks like she's hobbling. She didn't tell her mom. Maybe Casper is griping to his mom about living with a clumsy woman. No big deal."

I only vaguely hear Jack. I'm pulling up what few memories I have of Casper Wilson. Of course, no face comes to mind, but a couple vivid images flash across my mind's eye. Like the last time Casper and I were in the same place at the same time. That would be three years ago, at Casper's father's funeral.

I remember the funeral well, not just because it was only three years ago, but because Mr. Wilson was a massive, gigantic, no-holds-barred Green Bay Packer fan. His last wishes involved being buried in a Packer logo casket. He also requested the church choir learn the Green Packers' fight song (there is one). They sang while wearing green and gold choir gowns officially licensed by the NFL and including the Packers logo on the front and back of each gown. Believe me, Brenda Hill had plenty to say about that.

But Mr. Wilson was the richest man in church, so he got away with such less-than-respectful funeral requests. No one dared to make any critical comments within hearing of Mrs. Kimmy Wilson or either of her two sons.

Funny, how memory works. I haven't thought about Casper Wilson, or his older brother, Cooper, since the funeral. Suddenly that's all that's in my head.

Cooper, if I recall correctly, is a normal guy. He's older than Casper, I think he's a year older than I am. He was, at one point, one of the deacons my mother prayed would fall in love with me. Unfortunately for Mom's plans, Cooper Wilson left Wisconsin after he graduated from college and is now the Dean of Students at some upscale prep school in California. He's married and has three kids.

Anyway, turning my mental attention to Casper, I realize that the Wilson boys are shockingly dissimilar. Where Cooper graduated college, moved away, and is a success (at least, if you believe Mom when she's in one of her 'how will Nora ever get married when all the good men are gone' moods). On the other hand, Casper flunked out of at least three institutions of higher learning before moving back home to live with Kimmy and a houseful of hired help. That living arrangement ended when he married Cassie about a year ago. I remember Rose commenting that the idea of Casper Wilson marrying at all was a joke. Apparently he's a momma's boy who had no plans other than living off his inheritance.

Well, according to Rose, anyway. Of anyone in our family, she knows Casper best.

My eggs are getting cold, which is not a good thing for Eggs Benedict, so I return to eating, hoping that will help me ignore what's going on in my head. I no sooner manage to clean my plate and my brain when my phone buzzes. It's my mother.

Oh good.

At least she's texting me. That's a big deal for her, since she's all about that face to face conversation thing. "Tone of voice is the biggest part of the conversation, Nora," she would always say.

Since I don't always understand tone of voice, I really need the words to be the biggest part of any conversation. But that's just me.

"Your mom?" Jack looks up from his plate.

I want to laugh. "How did you know?"

"You've got that look on your face that you get when you're thinking about your mom."

It's a little scary, how well Jack seems to know me. Good thing he's on my side. "Yeah, she's just checking in on whether or not I've unraveled the mystery."

Jack pauses and gives me a wry grin. "Telling her about your gift probably didn't make your life any easier."

I shrug. "Not at the moment, no. She probably thinks I have it all figured out and I'm holding out on her to be dramatic."

"Think she'll ever understand?"

I shake my head. "Jack, I don't understand how it works, how can I expect Mom or my sisters to get it?"

"Huh." Jack makes a sort of surprised sound and returns his attention to his plate of food.

His vague syllable of surprise catches my notice. "Huh, what?"

"I'm sorry, what? Do you want some sugar for your coffee?" He hands me a paper packet of sugar.

I pause. I may have misunderstood what he was saying, or intending to say with that little grunt. And I realize that yes, I could use a bit of sugar. "You said something, just now."

"I did?"

"Yeah. You said, 'huh' like you were surprised."

"Oh. That. I didn't mean anything by that."

It's been my experience that when someone says they don't mean anything by something they say, they're not being truthful. "Jack, of course you meant something."

There's a strained pause between us and for one sick second I'm afraid this lovely brunch is going to deteriorate into an argument reminiscent of the one in Superior.

Fortunately for me, Jack is a grown up.

"I didn't mean anything bad, Nora. It's that you make this thing, this gift of yours way too complicated when it's not."

"Oh? Tell me, Mr. Terrell, how am I making this divine gift so complicated?" This should be good. I sit back and wait.

"You are able to find missing children. You hear a voice, you see a vision, whatever, but you're able to do it. You can't control the timing or anything, but it's not that complex really."

I think I'm starting to understand why Rose always grumbles about how her husband lives in a simple world full of simple answers. I always thought it would be cool to have quick, easy answers to stuff, but now, listening to Jack boil down to one sentence this ability I have, well, that's really annoying. And I would tell him that very thing, except...

Now is the time when I hear that little voice, the one I knew I would eventually hear. And this time I also get a vision, a photo clear image of Cassie and where she is at this moment.

Brunch is over.

I hate that I'm currently proving Jack right.

I throw a couple of twenties on the table and try to stand. Of course I fail at this move and Jack has to catch me, again.

It's a short hobble to the car, which is parked just outside in front of the restaurant. Jack helps me to the car without comment but I know him well enough to know he's probably trying to smother a chuckle. He sees to it that Mega-cast and I are settled before he asks anything. "So, where to? Are we going to check out that antique store up the street or..."

"Oh you know very well I just heard the voice and now we're going to go find Cassie...and rescue her unborn baby and all that." I'm sort of hoping they're both in the same place, of course. "We need to go to the parking lot behind the 217 building."

"Where's that?"

Jack doesn't know Waukesha, but I do. "East Park Street."

"She's there?"

I nod. "I don't think she's alone, either." The images I'm seeing are confusing, and, if I'm truly interpreting them correctly, disturbing. "We should hurry."

Waukesha is infamous for being a difficult town to drive in. I've never thought that. Well, until now when I'm trying to direct Jack through a couple narrow streets and around an extra block because of one way streets. Still, it only takes us a handful of minutes to get to East Park Street.

"The parking lot we want is up one block on our right." As I'm saying this, dark red sedan whizzes past us, going the wrong way. Jack swerves hard to the right to avoid a crash. In the process I smash my leg against the door and pain jolts all the way to my toes.

Jack glances in the rearview mirror. "I thought you said this was a one way street!" He's breathing heavily from a rush of adrenaline.

"It is!" I rub my knee as far down Megacast as I can reach. "That guy is going the wrong way."

"Some people." Jack makes a quick right hand turn. "We're here."

Immediately to our right, parked in the very back corner of the lot, are two vehicles. One is an older car, possibly as old my Forester, and possibly just as loved. The other is a large pickup truck, very shiny, very new.

"That's a new Ford Super Duty F-450 Platinum 4WD." Jack whistles softly.

"Fancy?"

He nods. "That truck starts at over seventy grand. The only guys I know who drive those are general contractors who are doing really well and need a ton of towing power." He squints. "I'm not seeing any kind of business name on the side of that."

"What does that mean?"

"Could mean the owner hasn't had time to get lettering put on. But it also could mean it belongs to some guy who wants to show off his money by buying a top of the line truck."

It seems like an unnecessary piece of information, but I have a sense that knowing about these two cars is going to be important. "What's the other car?"

"A twenty-year-old VW Passat. It's very nicely kept, but nowhere in the same class as the truck."

Sometimes it's great to have a car guy around. Knowing this about the two cars, I have to think that if Cassie is here, and my little voice is telling me she is, the VW is her ride. Sure, the rumor is that Casper is a wealthy guy. It's possible he bought his wife a giant truck. I shouldn't make assumptions about people. At least, that's what my mother keeps telling me.

Unfortunately for Mom, I've found my assumptions aren't often wrong.

I'm so wrapped up in my thoughts that I miss Jack getting out of the car until I hear my name.

"Nora! Nora Hill!"

It's not a man's voice. It's a woman's. I look out the window and see Jack reaching for a very pregnant woman as she crumples to the ground. I whip open my door and struggle to swing around and face them.

"Nora! It's me, Cassie! Cassie Wilson!"

"Cassie!" I struggle to stand, leaning heavily on the car door. "Cassie what happened?"

"There was a man. He…" She points to the truck and starts sobbing. "AGH!" She screams and holds her belly.

Jack is kneeling, cradling her head in his lap. "Nora, call 911," he says calmly. He's keeping his composure with Cassie screaming and I'm probably not looking my strongest. I can't stop staring at her. There are bruises on her arms and around her neck. There's a red mark around her left eye that looks like it's going to turn black soon enough. She's wearing a long tank top dress, not unusual for this weather, and her arms and shoulders are riddled with scrapes and cuts.

"Nora."

I blink my focus back to Jack. "Yes. I'm calling." I shove myself back into the car seat and fumble for my phone. I dial and give the operator our location. Within seconds I hear sirens.

"Cops will be here any minute, and an ambulance."

Cassie howls again.

106

There are about six feet between me and where Jack's kneeling. How I cover that distance without crutches I do not know, but the next thing I'm fully aware of is I'm the one sitting on the pavement, Cassie's head in my lap. I stroke her hair and mumble what I think are comforting words as I watch Jack get up and stride toward the truck.

The driver's door is open, so he doesn't have to touch anything to see what's going on in the front seat.

It's at that moment I see a rare shimmer of weakness in Jack Terrell. He takes one quick look into the front seat of that expensive truck. He steps back, turns his back to us, and vomits brunch into the tangled line of scrubby trees and bushes that outline the corner of the parking lot.

"Jack! What is it?"

He shouts something I don't understand and he heaves again but my attention is drawn back to Cassie because she is saying something I understand.

"Nora! I think my water just broke!"

I glance at the blacktop below the hem of her Capri pants and sure enough, it's wet.

Water.

I am exactly where I'm supposed to be.

I don't know how much time passes, maybe three minutes, maybe four, before two cop cars pull up to the lot. A heartbeat later a fire truck wails up the street, followed closely by an ambulance. Before I can gather my thoughts, the space around me is full of people. Normally I would be leaving the scene, but I can't. Cassie's head is still in my lap and every few minutes she tenses and bites back a scream. This is where I have to be, because this is where the baby is going to be in danger. This filthy corner of a shabby parking lot, lined with overgrown scrub trees and weeds, and shielded from the neighborhood's prying eyes only by a foul smelling industrial sized Dumpster, this is where this baby is threatening to be born so this is where I've been sent.

The EMTs kneel next to Cassie and I am ready to turn her over to professionals. I'm so ready, in fact, that I look over my shoulder at Jack and the cops. Well, I look at the cops in uniform and a guy I'm pretty sure is Jack. It's been a few minutes and Jack's face is again gone from my brain.

Jack is standing a respectful distance from the truck while a couple of cops look in the front seat. Much of the rescue personnel stay with their vehicles so they don't clutter the scene. Jack looks over at me and mouths one word, "Dead." Then he points his fingers to his head and makes a shooting motion.

"This baby is coming right now!"

I'm so engrossed is what's happening over my shoulder, the EMT's words barely register in my head. I turn my attention back to Cassie, who is now a stranger with her head in my lap. She's not biting back those screams anymore and the rescue team has broken out blankets and towels and sheets galore. Basically, from the belly down, Cassie is a tent.

"Well I'll just let you get to this," I try to shift out from under the weight of Cassie's head. Not sure what my plan is, since it's not likely I'm going to suddenly be able to stand up on my own.

"Don't leave me, Nora!" Cassie reaches up and grabs my arm.

I recall my brothers-in-law telling us how strong my sisters were during labor, how by simply holding hands they crushed fingers. I didn't understand that until this moment, when Cassie wraps her fingers around my arm and clamps down. Even without the Megacast, I wouldn't be able to break free.

"Stay where you are and keep your friend calm!" The female EMT barks at me.

Keep her calm? How am I supposed to do that? I'm not equipped for something like this. I'm supposed to find the missing child, which I have done, and then leave. This is the part where I leave.

"Okay, here we go! Give me a good, big push Cassie!" The male EMT says in a loud, yet somehow comforting, voice.

Cassie curls into a half sit-up and lets out a sound I do not recognize as human. She's still got a grip on my arm, which she tightens as she pushes. Fire shoots up to my shoulder and down to my elbow. "Breathe!" I yell, although I'm pretty sure I'm talking more to myself than to her.

"That's it, great! Now just one more!"

Cassie curls forward again and this time I join her howl. Maybe if we make enough noise this baby will shoot out of her and she'll stop trying to rip off my arm.

"Okay, hold it, hold it now," the female EMT says.

I don't know what they're doing on the other side of that tent and I don't think I want to. I look around. Weird, this little drama has drawn exactly zero bystanders. You'd think all the trucks and flashing lights and screaming would have attracted the attention of at least one casual observer. I mean, if a fire truck so much as slows down on my mother's street, everyone bolts out of their houses and stands on the sidewalk to wait and see what's happening. It's the only time the lady two doors down from Mom comes out of her house.

But here, on this one way street behind a row of office buildings and businesses, there's no one. I look across the street at the aging houses, once glorious Victorians now divided into ill-kept low rent apartments. If anyone is witnessing what's happening in this parking lot, they are doing so from behind drawn curtains.

"There we go, Cassie! A baby boy!"

The sound of a new baby's mew shakes me out of my thoughts. The male EMT is holding a bloody towel, which I think is silly, until I realize that there's a face poking out of that towel.

Cassie is panting and crying and laughing all at once. She finally relaxes against my lap, her whole body limp from the exertion.

"Wow, Cassie, look what you did," I say lamely. "That's your baby."

"Oh Nora, thank you!"

"For what?"

She holds my hand and smiles. "I couldn't have done this without you and your friend over there."

I'm fairly certain she could have, but I'm not going to argue with a woman who just pushed a person out of her body and lived to tell about it. I keep her hand in mine. I don't want to let go. This connection I have with Cassie in this moment is real, it's got a pulse. I've made a friend, right here in this parking lot. I don't want to lose that.

Ultimately, I do have to let go as the EMTs work on mother and baby. It takes a few minutes for them to get Cassie and the infant loaded onto a gurney and packed into the ambulance. The male EMT very nicely grabs my crutches out of the car and helps me to a standing position before they take off, sirens blaring. The fire truck follows them away from the scene.

"They're going to be a while," Jack walks up to me and nods in the direction of the pick-up. "You want to see if it's Casper?"

I don't have to remind Jack how dumb that question is. He realizes it immediately. Besides, the cops have taped off a huge square around both vehicles so I couldn't even get close enough to get a real look if I wanted to. Which I don't. I'm not a fan of looking at dead people.

"We should get you out of this heat," he says. "And get out of their way so they can do their work." He points to the cops who are collecting evidence and taking pictures.

Jack helps me turn toward the car, but of course then we're looking directly at the spot where Cassie just gave birth. The pavement is gooey and red, like someone spilled paint. Then I realize that's all from Cassie.

111

I feel lightheaded. Jack puts a firm hand on my shoulder to steady me.

"We have a few questions, if you don't mind," one of the cops comes up to us.

"Is it okay if I sit in the car while you ask me?" I don't have much patience with police. It's not that I don't like them; they have a job to do just like anyone else. It's just that typically if I'm being questioned by police it's because I managed to find a child no one else could and, well, that raises suspicions about my involvement.

In this case the police ask a handful of questions about the scene when we got there. I'm not terribly helpful, not because I don't want to be, but because they started off with, "How did Mrs. Wilson look when you got here?"

I don't know how she looked because I didn't know it was her. This fact I explain to the officer who realizes that I'm going to be a horrible eye witness. The officers turn their attention and most of their questions to Jack.

It's strange, but I sense Jack isn't telling them everything he knows. He's holding back, although he's doing it smoothly enough the cops don't catch on. After talking to him for a few more minutes, one of the officers gives Jack his card and says, "If you remember anything else, this is my number."

"Okay, let's get out of here." Jack settles me into the car and hurries around the front to his seat so he can crank up the AC.

It takes a moment for the icy air to filter through the vents, but it's a beautiful moment when it does. We drive to the end of the block and across the street to the library

112

parking lot. Jack leaves the car running, but gets out, pulls out his phone and immediately makes a call. I'm guessing he's calling Sam.

I watch him talk on the phone, but I don't hear much. The Cassie Wilson drama is put on the back burner when I remember why it is he's here in the first place. A tiny bit of panic twinges inside me. If Jack has to go back to Manitowoc today, and he's moving to St. Louis soon, what if I never see him again?

This thought takes my internal feelings from quiver of panic to shards of glass in my gut.

I'm not sure which is more surprising; the fact that I've grown attached to anyone enough to care whether or not they're around, or that it's Jack that's causing this internal upheaval. I mean, sure, I had a crush on him back in high school, who didn't? He was Mr. All American.

Granted he did tell me he cared for me yesterday, which is new territory for me. No man, other than my father, ever said much in the way of affection to or about me. I'm not blaming the few guys I've dated for that. I mean, it's hard to develop feelings of a positive nature for someone who, on the first date, forgets what you look like when she comes back from the ladies' room, sits at another table and winds up actually being on a date with someone else.

I mean, I thought it was sort of funny, but apparently neither my original date, who had to pay for my dinner, nor my second date's girlfriend saw the humor in it. Imagine the look on her face, when she got back from the restroom and found me sitting in her seat having a lovely time.

At least I killed two birds with one stone on that one. Neither guy called me back. I'm not exactly second date material.

So yes, knowing that Jack cares about me is unnerving because I don't know what my response should be. I just know that the idea of him walking out of my world, and taking Sam with him, is not pleasant.

While I'm trying to sort out the pile of rubble that is my romantic self, Jack gets back in the car. "Sam says hi. Mary Jo does, too."

I'd forgotten that Sam was staying with MaryJo. "You called to tell her that you're…"

"Probably going to be home later today than expected." He stares out the window. "So, about Cassie…"

"Oh yeah. How about Cassie? Having the baby in that gross parking lot." A shiver runs up my arms when I think of her howls with each contraction. Maybe it's a good thing I'm not anyone's idea of a second date. I doubt I'd be on board with having kids. Not if labor is anything like what I just witnessed.

"That building is where Casper works?"

I shrug. "I guess."

"Why would he be there on a Sunday?"

I glance at Jack. "Why would you be asking me these questions?"

He inhales and holds his breath for a moment, the exhales like he's getting rid of something foul inside of his lungs. "When we got there, what did Cassie look like?"

"I covered this with the cops. I haven't a clue."

"No, I don't mean her face. I mean…what did her body look like?"

I close my eyes. The image of her arms and shoulders is clear. "She looked like she'd been beaten up."

"Right. Lots of bruises and scrapes, right?"

"Yeah."

"Did she say anything to you?"

"You mean beyond asking me not to leave her and then screaming her lungs out?" I shake my head. "No."

"But her mom called your mom yesterday, right? Asked if she thought everything was okay?"

"Right. Jack, what are you getting at?"

He shakes his head. "I'm not sure. Do you think we can go back to the parking lot and just take a look around?"

"I suppose. Although it's a good bet the cops are still there."

"Yeah, you're probably right. But I still want to take a look at the lot."

"Fine. Just remember, it's a one way street, we have to go around the block."

Jack eases the Forester out of the library lot. "The bruises and scrapes on Cassie. Did they look…" he stops.

Oh my goodness! It's worse than waiting for Rose's four year old to pick a candy bar at the store! He's obviously trying to get to something, but I don't know what. "Looked how, Jack? How did they look? Gross? Bloody? Dirty?"

"Old." He says the word slowly, quietly, as if to combat my barrage of volume.

"Old?"

He shakes his head. "I'm sure I wasn't seeing things right, but think about this: Casper goes to his office on a Sunday, maybe to work on something. Cassie shows up…who knows why. But they both park in the corner farthest from the door."

Yeah, that's weird. I'll give Jack points for that.

"So they park there and maybe someone comes up, and it's like a robbery or something. Maybe Cassie gets there first and the robber beats her up, and then Casper pulls in and sees this and is going to get out of the truck and save her, but the robber shoots him."

"But doesn't take anything?"

Jack nods. "You see my problem?"

"Who said it was a robber?"

"You didn't listen to the questions the cops asked me?"

"No. I zoned out." I can feel a wave of disappointment waft off of him. "Hey it's really hot out here and I'd just watched a woman give birth in a parking lot.

116

Cut me some slack if I don't analyze questions someone else is asking you."

"Fine, fine. Whatever. The point is, the cops seem to be working on this idea that a random guy was beating Cassie and then shot Casper and took off."

We round the corner back onto East Park Street. I study each house as we roll by. There is no one outside, no one sitting on any porches. The street is a ghost town. "Not a lot in the way of neighborhood witnesses."

"Not really."

"You didn't tell the cops about the car going the wrong way."

Jack pulls into the lot, stopping the car several yards away from where police personnel are still gathering bits and pieces from the scene. "No. I did not."

"Why not?"

He squints at the corner where the two vehicles are still parked. "I don't know. But look, the way the scrub trees and the Dumpster sort of act like wall around that corner?"

"Yeah."

"So, if no one's in those buildings," he points to the office building and the two buildings on either side. One is a restaurant that is only open in the evenings. The other is an adult day care facility that's not open on Sundays. "Then no one from that direction saw anything. And no one driving up the street would see anything because this corner is completely hidden from view."

I suddenly something. "You know, my brother-in-law Scott once told me a story about this parking lot."

"Really? A story about this specific lot?"

Wait, that was sarcasm coming from Jack, right? So maybe I do recognize tones in peoples' voices. "Scott swore me to secrecy about this. No one else in the family knows this story."

"About this parking lot."

I nudge his elbow. "Do you want to hear it or not?"

"Go ahead."

"Thank you. Okay, so remember like some fifteen, sixteen years ago, when the whole state was up in arms about the deer population having some kind of brain disease?"

Jack shakes his head and smiles. "I can't wait to hear how you connect the tragedy in this parking lot and Chronic Wasting Disease."

"Well I will if you would let me finish." I take a breath. I can't believe I remember this story, or that Scott trusted me enough to tell me. I guess he needed to tell someone, ease his conscience with confession, that sort of thing. And he told the one relative who wouldn't rat him out to his wife. "Anyway, so Scott had gotten a deer during hunting season the year before, and the freezer was full of venison. But Rose read something like a hundred articles about how eating meat tainted with CWD would cause all kinds of health problems in children."

"I remember. I had to dispose of a couple deer myself."

"Well, so did Scott. Rose told him to get rid of the meat. So he packed it up in his car and took it to the closest place he could think of where no one would care what he was dumping." I point to the Dumpster. "That Dumpster, right there. He told me he tossed more than a hundred pounds of meat in the middle of a summer day. He said he parked the car right there, next to those trees and tossed everything right into the Dumpster without anyone seeing anything or saying anything."

"Well it's not like he could be positive no one saw anything."

"True, but Scott always said he thought he could have dumped a body in there and no one would have noticed. He told me he drove by a couple days later. The Dumpster hadn't been emptied yet, but the meat had thawed. He said the smell was spectacular, it was so strong."

Jack studies the corner of the lot again. "It is pretty secluded. And it's a one way street, so there's no view of the corner of the lot if you drive the right way…and no one would be driving the other way."

"Except that one person who almost hit us." I'm surprised at how excited I am. I never really want to figure out the why of it all. Once I find a kid I'm done. I'm out. I don't want to get more involved. Call it self-preservation.In my experience, the only thing that comes of digging deeper is a lot of ugliness. But here, it feels like we have a happy ending. I mean, not for Casper so much, sure, but Cassie had her baby, so that's a happy thing. Right? "Did you see if it was a man or a woman?"

"I didn't see either way. I was trying to keep us from being killed."

"Good thing you didn't mention it to the cops, then."

"But maybe I should." He turns off the car and opens his door. "You want to come with me?"

No. I don't. I want to go home and lie down. But I can't say that. Jack's obviously having some crisis of conscience here and I should be supportive. It's what any good...what any good person who might be interested in someone in an ever so slightly romantic way would do.

But I also don't want to slow him down. "Just get me out of the car so I'm not sitting in the heat."

"Good plan. This could take a while." He helps me out, props me against the front corner of the passenger side of the car, and gives me my crutches to lean on. Then he walks over to the men in blue, gets their attention, and starts talking.

SUNDAY 12:30 PM

Jack walks away and I stare at the place where we found Cassie. I try to picture the scene Jack painted: a pregnant woman, recently attacked by someone who also shot her husband. That seems logical, albeit odd for Waukesha, a town known more for its twisted traffic patterns and quirky inhabitants than for its violent crimes.

The two vehicles are still there, although I'm sure the police department will tow them away soon. I can see logic in how the cars are parked. The scrub trees are the only bit of shade in this whole lot. It would make sense that the Wilsons would park there, in an attempt to keep the vehicles slightly cooler than if they were in the sun. Maybe if Casper was coming to catch up on some work, Cassie wanted to come to the office as well, spend some time tidying his space or whatever it is wives do.

That truck, though. It's really new. It's the kind of new where the owner would park miles away from any other car rather than run the risk of having someone ding the doors. Casper, what I remember of him, strikes me as an owner like that.

I remember my sisters being really surprised when he got married. Casper wasn't, as they put it, a person who thought much of other people. Unless he was the person he was thinking about. Then he thought plenty.

Maybe Cassie wasn't going to Casper's office with him. Maybe she had a shift at the deli.

No, that can't be. The Rochester Deli isn't open on Sundays.

So they came in separate cars and parked inches away from each other in a fairly secluded spot.

I try to picture this in my mind. If Cassie pulls in first, and the mystery assailant attacks her, that would mean Casper parked his truck while Cassie was attacked.

What kind of heartless demon could watch his pregnant wife being beaten and still park his truck so perfectly?

If Casper pulled into the lot first, then the assailant shot him and then attacked Cassie, not with a gun, but with fists.

That doesn't make sense either.

My phone rings, which startles me and I jump a tiny bit, destabilizing the crutches and tipping to one side. I catch myself before I fall, but I jar my cast just enough to send shockwaves of pain up and down my leg. I should let it just go to voicemail, while I'm standing here, howling in pain, but instead, I answer it. "WHAT?"

"Well good morning to you, too, Sunshine."

I wince a few times, willing away the worst of the anguish. "Connie. Aren't you an hour ahead of me? Shouldn't you be saying, 'good afternoon' instead?"

"When one doesn't get to bed until four AM because one was at a book release party for John Grisham, one does not rise before noon, or, in fact, before two or three. Unfortunately for me, your mother still thinks I'm some sort of medical professional and therefore I keep nurses' hours, which is to say I'm on call day or night." Connie pauses before continuing with her rant. "Which, as you know, I am not."

I have nothing to say I have nothing to say in defense of myself. Again, I realize my life is over, thanks to that deadly combination of my mother's hoarding habit and the fact that I lost my phone in her pile of junk. I'm going to have to explain things to Mom soon, or Connie is going to dump me as a client and then I'll have to break in a new agent. I don't have that kind of energy.

"Connie, I'm so sorry about my mom. She's…well, she's…"

"She's a pain in my neck, is what she is, Nora. Do you know why she called me today? Do you have any idea why she woke me from a lovely slumber?"

I'm not sure I want to know. I'm mentally doing a run-down of possible reasons why Brenda Hill could have made a Sunday morning contact with Connie. I've got nothing. "Go ahead, Connie. Why did my mother call you?"

"You know very well why, and I can't believe I have to hear it from her and not you."

I almost think Connie sounds genuinely hurt, which is weird. Over the years we've given each other plenty of grief, both joking and serious, and not once have I ever gotten the feeling that anything could insult her. "What are you talking about, Connie?" I am getting a strange, twisted feeling in my stomach.

"Your mother wants to congratulate you. Would you answer her calls just once so I can get some sleep? And also, hey, congrats. I'm shocked, but congrats."

What is Connie talking about? Why would Mom call Connie today? I'm in town. I'm two miles from her kitchen! I check my phone…sure enough…I've got four missed calls and a pile of texts. Looks like I accidentally put it on silence when I called the ambulance.

"Nora!"

I shake myself out of my thoughts and focus on Connie's angry voice. "Okay, okay, I missed a couple calls from her. Was she worried I'd wandered off again? I mean, I am with…a friend."

"A friend? That's what you're calling him?"

"Um, yeah. Jack's a friend."

"There's a better word for someone like Jack, Nora. You're a writer, you should know the word."

At this point I'm completely and utterly in the weeds as to what she's trying to tell me. Normally conversations with Connie are straightforward and clear. "Connie, can you give up the righteous indignation thing you've got going on here and just spit out what you mean?"

"You could stop being obtuse, you know. It's not like it's a secret. I mean, he asked you during brunch, right?"

What is she talking about? Did Mom tell Connie about my gift and that I was looking for a missing pregnant woman who might not even be missing? It's possible, I wouldn't put it past Mom. But why would Connie congratulate me for that? It's not like I've had a chance to call anyone about finding Cassie. "I gotta be honest, Connie. I have no idea what you're saying to me."

Connie grunts angrily. "Look you don't want to tell me anything, that's fine. I'll find out when I find out. Just make sure the cake is really good, otherwise I'm not leaving New York for the reception. Meanwhile, tell your mother I'm not your babysitter, and get me some new pages!" She ends the call before I can respond.

I feel like she and my mother are in on some joke and I don't know anything about it.

I glance at Jack, who's finished his conversation with the police and is walking over to me. And then I'm struck by lightning. Not literally, of course. Figuratively.

I know the word Connie was hinting at.

Fiancé.

Jack was going to ask me to marry him? That's why Mom called Connie?

Stunned at the thought, I slip my phone back into my pants pocket. Or, at least I try to. What I manage to do, however, is miss the pocket and drop my phone into the slender gap between Megacast and my leg. I try to reach into the cast to retrieve the phone, but in the process one of my crutches clatters to the ground and the other one slips under the sudden shift in my weight and I hit the concrete. I hit it hard.

So this is what it's like to black out from a head injury.

I'm not sure how long I'm out. I open my eyes and I'm lying on my side. My leg is throbbing and I'm thoroughly aware of the pain in my head. But none of that is as important as the image of a woman driver in a large sedan wheeling past us going the wrong way.

"What do you mean, 'woman driver?'"

I look sideways and upward at whom I am assuming is Jack. I didn't realize I'd said anything out loud.

"Nora, it's Jack. You don't need to shout. I can hear you."

That's the thing I really like about Jack. He always tells me his name if he's been out of my sight for a few minutes. It's nice.

"Thank you. It's just good manners."

Seriously, am I having a conversation I'm not aware of? I still haven't said a word."

"Yes, you have, and you're shouting."

Jack helps me sit up and that's when I become solidly aware of a ringing in my ears. A gentle, deep toll of a church bell. Nope, I've got the tinny jangle of ten thousand toy tambourines going on. Sort of like the Christmas morning, when all the kids were little and Lily thought it would be amusing to give all the grandchildren tiny percussion instruments. The kids had a blast. Rose and Lily and Mom laughed at the magnificent musical delights the precocious angels were making. The brothers-in-law were glad no one was fighting, so they loved it.

Guess who wanted to go hide in a small, dark place, far away from everything.

So the noise going on in my head is that.

"Yeah. Is your head okay?" Jack keeps a hand on my shoulder to steady me.

I touch a tender spot at the back of my head. There's the start of a nice bump back there.

"Nora? Nora?"

Jack and I blink at each other. It takes both of us a moment to realize that the faint voice we're hearing is coming from my phone, which has, inexplicably, worked its way halfway down my cast. On the inside.

I now have giant talking leg.

"Nora, you called me back. What do you want?"

I must have pocket dialed Connie. Or should we call this leg dialing? Look, I've now created a new social faux pas. Good for me. "Connie! I'm going to have to call you back!" I shout as loud as I can.

"Fine, whatever!" Connie's angry, but muffled, retort emits from just below my knee.

Jack stands and grins at me. "I'll ask about this Connie person later. Right now, we need to get to the hospital."

"Why?"

"Because that's what people do when they black out after fall. They go to the hospital."

"I black out all the time, you know. It's not like this is new for me."

"Yes, but your head hit the pavement really hard. I don't want to take any chances. You were shouting and not making sense. That's not a good thing."

"First of all, Jack, I wasn't talking out loud."

"You were," he hoists me to a standing position and props a crutch under each arm. "You were shouting something about a woman driver."

"Oh, that. Well, yeah. That driver that was going the wrong way. It was a woman."

He doesn't seem convinced. "How would you have seen that? And how would you have recognized that?"

With a big sigh, I try to hold on to my patience. "First of all, I can tell the difference between men and women. Second…" I pause, realizing my righteous indignation is about to evaporate. "Second I just saw her in my brain."

Jack nods as if he completely understands what I mean. "Like one of your visions, right?"

Sure. Let's go with that.

"Or maybe you have a concussion." He starts moving me into the car.

I hate not having complete control over my body. People get to just move me around like a piece of furniture. It's not as fun as it sounds. "I'm an adult, Jack. You can't make me go see a doctor."

He grins. "No?"

"No."

"Okay. Well how about if we go see how Cassie and the baby are doing?"

I sense I'm being trapped into something, but I really do want to see that baby. I bet he's a little cuter now. They've probably cleaned all the goo off of him. "Okay. We can go see Cassie."

"And if we happen to bump into a doctor along the way, maybe we have him or her just take a tiny peek at your head." Jack says this while buckling my seatbelt.

"You just used your dad powers on me, didn't you?"

"Something like that." He closes my door, rounds the front of the car, and gets in his side.

My head is splitting. It might be a good idea to have someone double check that I don't have a brain injury. A girl like me can really only deal with so much brain stuff at once, and I'm pretty sure I have everything I can handle.

SUNDAY 3:00 PM

It's been said, and more than a few times, that man plans and God laughs. This I believe without any reservation. Any time I think my life is going in one direction God points His finger at me and whispers, "ka-pow," or something of that nature and my world develops wrinkles I never saw coming.

Like Jack. Jack's a wrinkle. I had no intention of spending more time in Manitowoc than it took to drive through it, but my car broke down and I met Jack, my high school crush, and wound up going to my high school reunion. Jack, in turn, introduced me to another wrinkle, his daughter Samantha, who convinced Jack to drive her across the state from Manitowoc to Superior to help me locate a missing child. And it was in Superior where Jack and I had the big fight about whether or not I was mother figure material.

This is what's running through my mind as Jack's driving me to Waukesha Memorial Hospital. Putting the bits and pieces of my phone conversation together, I have to believe that Mom and Connie think Jack proposed to me. However, unless I missed something, that hasn't happened.

I can't blame him for deciding against it. Maybe picking me up after yet another black out reminded him how high maintenance I am. Granted this time it was a fall, but the fact remains, I black out more frequently than your average girl.

Who wants to make a life with a woman who may, or may not, black out while driving a car? It's not like I have epilepsy…there's no pill to stave off Divine Ka-pows. A guy can't hitch himself to a girl who can't be depended on to remain conscious.

Maybe his change of heart is the result of something else. Maybe Mary Jo told him what I do for a living and he's cheesed at me because I could very well have bailed him out of his financial mess and since I didn't he now thinks I'm holding back my help because I'm selfish or I don't like him or whatever.

I can't blame him for any of those arguments.

Jack parks at the emergency entrance. By the time he's come around to my door, I've convinced myself that the very best thing in the world for him, and for me, is if we never see each other again.

I'm really good at torpedoing anything that might give me happiness.

Who can blame me? The world has not exactly been kind to me and every insult, every moment of mocking laughter, every thin thread of friendship that's been shredded has served to build armor around my heart. I've convinced myself that Jack wants to dump me off and race away. Honestly this makes that whole thing about moving to St. Louis way easier. I mean, there's zero temptation to even think about breaking my self-imposed exile from the city. So that's a good thing, right?

So why is there a tear in the corner of my eye?

Allergies. Sudden, immediate, adult onset allergies. That's the only answer I'm going to accept for that question.

Jack taps on the window. It's still pretty cool in the car and I know it's blazing how outside so I don't open the door. "Nora, I'm going to get a wheelchair. Stay put."

Where does he think I'm going to go? And how does he think I'm going to get there?

Jack may be out of my sight, but he's not out of my thoughts. I think about how he's been, since we reconnected earlier this summer. He's been kind to me, helpful. A really good partner. With the exception of our argument about whether or not I'd be a good role model for Sam, he's been…well he's been everything.

He's been great. I'm the one who's the problem.

There's a tap on the window. "Nora, it's me, Jack."

I open the door and the sticky heat envelops me. This only serves to put me in an even darker mood. I do almost nothing to help him situate me and Mega-cast in the wheelchair. While he's kneeling in front of me, hoisting Mega-cast onto the footrest, I begin what I believe is going to be the final battle. Once this conversation is over, everything will be on the table. He won't ask me to marry him or to move to St. Louis. I'll be free from the thought of a normal, happy life. And things can go back to the way they were, before I got stuck in Manitowoc.

Ah, the good old days.

"Look, Jack, if you maybe shouldn't have told everyone you were going to propose to me. You know, since you haven't."

He looks at me with those beautiful blue eyes of his, and I know he's not going to lie to me. So this is either going to be really painful or really great.

I know how this is going to go.

"What in the world are you talking about, Nora?" He remains kneeling, even though both of my feet are secured and I'm ready to roll. Literally.

"I mean, Jack, that I had this super strange conversation with Connie today, and she seems to think you're going to ask me something important. Why would you tell everyone? And it's now obvious that you are not going to ask me because you've decided, once again, that I'm not good enough. Which is fine. I already know I'm not good enough."

There. I told him.

Jack shakes his head. "I don't know anyone named Connie."

He's stalling. Okay, I'll play along. "You talked to my mother who talked to Connie. At any rate, Connie knows and she's congratulating me for something I don't believe has happened."

"Who is Connie?" Jack holds up his hands like he's praying.

He's still stuck on that? My patience has run out. "Connie is my agent!"

"Why do you have an agent?"

We've enter the ER and the sudden chill wakes us to the reality that we are both shouting. The waiting room is crowded and every single head in the place turns and stares at us. I take a breath, and so does Jack, and on the exhale we're both laughing. It's uncomfortable, but it's laughter and it propels us away from a conversation that was not going to end well otherwise.

We break away from the conversation long enough to check in with the ER desk nurse. She asks us the nature of my injury, all the while staring at my leg.

"I fell," I try to explain.

"And she broke her brain."

I can't believe Jack is being sassy with the nurse. I can't contain the blast of laughter that flies out of my mouth. The nurse frowns at us, quite possibly not seeing the humor.

"Take a seat, someone will call you in a moment."

Jack and I survey the packed waiting area. I know I want to let out another guffaw. There's no way anyone is seeing us in a moment. Unless that moment is actually a month long.

133

"We should probably settle down and find a seat," he says before clearing his throat in a way that indicates he, too, would really like to laugh out loud.

Jack parks me, in the wheelchair, and sits next to me. "Okay seriously, how about if you and I get on the same page? Start with Connie."

I tell Jack about Connie, about my books, and about how I want to pay off his debts so he can stay in Manitowoc because there's no way on earth I'm going to St. Louis. I tell him everything he doesn't already know about me. I leave nothing out. I go right up to the point where Connie congratulates me for a reason I don't understand, and how my mother is in on it, but how I'm certain it's a misunderstanding.

"It's not a misunderstanding."

Jack's tone is so low I nearly miss what he's telling me. "I'm sorry…what now?"

Jack pats my hand. "You mother…she didn't misunderstand."

I feel like I'm on the other side of a mirror. Nothing makes sense. The idea that Jack is going to propose to me is ridiculous. I mean, Jack's never even tried to kiss me. Isn't some sort of kissing or attempting to kiss supposed to be part of a courtship?

Courtship? What, he's going to woo me? We live in the 1920's? No, wait, we live in the early 1700's and he wants to arrange a marriage between us and he needed my mother's permission.

Is that how arranged marriages even work?

134

"If you recall, I started that conversation when we were on your mom's porch talking about St. Louis." He shrugs. "I really wanted to wait for the right moment, even if it means waiting a long time for you to get past…being you." He grins at me. "I told Sam that. I told her this was not something that was positively happening this weekend, and I told her not to say anything to anyone until I had actually asked you. But what she heard was, 'Tell everyone I'm proposing today.' She must have talked to your mom."

"Right, right. You just haven't found the right moment." I'm frantically thumbing through my mental rolodex for some sort of road map that might make this conversation less awkward. Unfortunately I write adventure books for young boys. I don't deal in matters of the heart. Well, unless it's the hero piercing the heart of a swamp monster or something like that.

I'm not completely certain Jack and I are even talking about the same thing. I would stop him and ask for clarification, but this is one of those conversations that has now gone on too long for anyone to back track. Maybe if I keep agreeing with him, he'll get around to telling me precisely what we're discussing.

"Exactly. Unfortunately, Sam can't keep a secret. She told Mary Jo and MaryJo must have called your mother. Or Sam called your mother."

"Sam does have Mom's number." It all makes sense now, and it all comes back to me losing my phone. Once again, I'll beat myself up for that mistake.

"Right. Now the connection between your mom and Connie…"

I sigh. "Mom thinks Connie's like my nurse or something."

"So you haven't told your family what you do for a living?"

"No."

"Don't you think maybe you should? Maybe that might make your relationship more…more…"

"Normal?"

He grins. "You said it I didn't. But yeah. Maybe if they knew you could take care of yourself just fine, maybe they would stop treating you like a mental patient."

I'm not sure whether to laugh or be indignant and before I can make a decision, the ER doors slide open.

"That's Casper's mother," Jack whispers. "She looks terrible."

I'm sure she does. Her son has just been murdered. Who on earth knows what they told her to get her to come to the hospital.

Mrs. Wilson spends a very short amount of time at the desk with the humor-deficient nurse before another mirthless woman comes out and walks her down a hall and out of our sight.

I can't know what she's feeling, but Jack's hand tenses on my arm as he watches her. He's relating to her as a parent. I close my eyes. If anything happened to Sam…I open my eyes quickly, erasing the thought.

The door swishes open again and it's another woman. She's not whispering, which is helpful to those of us sitting here waiting for something to happen.

"I'm Janet Keen. I believe they brought my daughter, Cassie Wilson, here? I was told to come to this hospital."

Humor-deficient is helpful, and also not quiet. "Yes, Mrs. Keen. Cassie's not in the ER. She's been moved to the maternity floor. She's in room 417. You go through those doors there…" the nurse gives detailed directions that I'm really hoping Jack hears because she lost me at "maternity floor."

"Hey," I poke Jack's arm. "Let's just go up to maternity, see Cassie and the baby, and get out of here and go get some pizza or something. Sound good?"

Jack grins. "We can do that."

"Really?"

"Just one tiny change: First we'll have someone look at your head. Then the rest of it."

Obviously he's the smarter of the two of us. "Fine, fine." I cross my arms, trying to look angry.

"I'm going to see if I can find some coffee. Do you want some?"

As much as I love coffee, hospital coffee, in my book, ranks right down there with beets, dead birds on the sidewalk, and any conversation with my mother that involves the words, 'women's problems.' But, it doesn't look like we're going anywhere anytime soon and coffee

137

might be a nice diversion. "Sure, if you find some. Just bring some sugar along, just in case it's gross."

"Understood. I won't be long. You...stay here and stay out of trouble."

"What kind of trouble could I possibly get into?" I watch him head down a long and shiny hallway until one of those heavy hydraulic doors hisses shut behind him.

I glance at the TV. It's one of those home improvement shows where a person who needs six closets just for her shoes decides she wants to live in a 200 square foot house. So a crew of people build her this tiny home where she has to climb up a narrow ladder to get to her bed, and the height of her "bedroom" is roughly four feet, which means she'll never sit up and read in bed because the ceiling is too low. My favorite part of those shows is when she tells the builders she needs a ton of closet space and they build her a cubby the size of a shoe box. I would love to see the follow up on those homes, like six months later. Are the people still living in that teeny tiny space, or have they come to their senses and moved into a proper house?

And yes, these musings are coming from the same person who pretty much lives in her car.

"Nora? Nora Hill?"

The smooth tone of a man's voice breaks into my thoughts on tiny homes. I don't want to acknowledge him. I want to sit here, alone, without having to deal with social awkwardness.

Against my better judgment I turn and look in the direction of the voice. "I'm sorry?" Behind me stand a very tall man. He's thin, pretty well built, and has a nice tan. I'm going to go ahead and say he's a good looking guy, even if his face means nothing to me.

"Oh, Nora, it's so nice to see a familiar face."

Well, good looking tall guy, I wish I could say the same thing.

"Do you mind if I sit down?"

What I want to say is, why on earth would someone like you want to sit next to a purple haired freak show like me?

What I actually say is, "Sure. Go ahead."

This concussion thing is making me polite. I don't like it.

"I don't know if you remember me, I'm Cooper Wilson, Casper's older brother?"

Okay, now I have my bearings. Kimmy Wilson just walked in here. Cooper must be in town visiting and came in when they called about Casper.

"I was looking…for my mom." He takes a breath, like he's trying to hold in a sneeze. Only I'm pretty sure it's not a sneeze.

I'm at a loss for the right thing to say. "I'm glad you're able to be here, Cooper. I...I thought you were living in California?"

"I am. We're still on summer break, so I was home visiting. My wife and kids couldn't get away."

That's all the casual chit chat I've got. "Ah. Okay then."

My mom or my sisters would be able to engage Cooper in conversation that would be helpful and comforting. Unfortunately for Cooper, I'm the Hill he's sitting next to in this moment of sorrow.

Cooper continues the conversation, much to my shock. "They say it was a random attack. That you and your friend found them in a parking lot?"

I nod. "We did. My friend Jack and I found them. Jack's out getting coffee right now, so that's why he's not here." Man, do I sound callous. I'm terrible. I'm a terrible person who should not be allowed to talk to people.

But now I'm wonder how much the cops told Mrs. Wilson. If they didn't tell her Casper's dead...then I do not want to be the one to break it to Cooper. I haven't a clue what cops do in cases like this.

"I'm so sorry...about this." I do my best to sound sympathetic.

"Thanks." He reaches down and hugs me before sitting in the chair next to me. I glance around, really wishing Jack would show up. How long does it take to find coffee in a hospital anyway?

But here I am, sitting next to Cooper Wilson. I know his brother is dead, and I know his nephew is born. I don't know if Cooper knows either of those two bits of information. I also don't know why he's sitting next to me instead of locating his mother who is, no doubt, getting some bad news even as we speak.

Adults make no sense. At least with kids, it's not hard to figure out why they do something. Believe it or not, kids are pretty logical, very 'point A to point B' sort of people. Adults are different.

This is probably why I write for children. I don't like spending time in the adult world. Adults are mean to each other for no reason other than they can be. Anyone who says, "kids are cruel" either hasn't been paying attention or doesn't understand the meaning of the word "cruel." Sure, kids mock, bully, belittle and hurt other kids. I'm not denying it. It's an imperfect world, full of sin. But the difference comes in the amount of damage a child can and will do at his or her worst as opposed to the pain an adult can inflict on someone on the most normal Tuesday.

I can't focus on Cooper, however. Something's stuck in my brain. Cassie Wilson was beaten. Casper was shot. I just don't think the same person did damage to both Wilsons.

And then there's something else: Janet Keen called my mother last night to ask her if she thought Cassie was okay. That's when I blacked out, even though, Cassie wasn't missing. So it wasn't about Cassie being missing...it was about her being in danger or her baby being in danger.

In danger from what? They were in the parking lot of Casper's office. It's Sunday. It's broad daylight. It's Waukesha.

I just can't buy the idea of a random attacker.

A different, darker thought creeps into my head. Yes, adults are far more evil to each other than children ever could be. Most of the time they're just better at hiding the cruelty under cover of "It's just business" or "I was kidding!"

I stare at Cooper, wondering what questions are running through his head. Undoubtedly, he knew Casper better than anyone, except possibly Cassie.

He doesn't seem to be in a rush to join his mom. Neither of us speaks for what feels like a really, really long time. I shift in my wheelchair, wondering about Jack and the coffee. I mean, it's a hospital. Looking around I see at least three different coffee stations for people in the waiting room.

And Jack, oddly enough, walked right past all of them.

This is the guy who wants me to upheave my life and move to St. Louis and be...be what? His neighbor? His...nanny?

His wife?

How can I consider moving down there at his request for any reason when he can't manage to get me a cup of coffee in under an hour. I mean, it would have taken me less time to fly down to Columbia or where ever they're growing coffee beans these days, harvest some beans fly them back up here, milk a cow, for cream, you know, and make the stupid coffee.

And he wants me to move down to St. Louis.

Well, I suppose I get it. Anyone who would take this long to locate coffee in a place where there are pots of the stuff every seven feet...yeah, he might need an extra pair of hands, someone more observant and organized, to help guide Sam to adulthood.

Guide Sam to adulthood? What is going on in my brain right now? Who talks like that? I don't talk like that.

"You know, Casper never really wanted children. I wonder how Cassie convinced him to have one."

I blink myself back to the present because, seriously, I was so wrapped in my own thoughts, I forgot Cooper was there.

"You really don't need to hear this." Cooper says.

Yes, yes, I do need to hear this. I need to iron out all the wrinkles in this mess so I can file it away behind a door in my mental hallway.

"He was way too young for that kind of responsibility."

Casper is a year younger than I am, and both of us are well beyond the description of "young."

I don't need to read Cooper's expression to know he'd be in agreement if I were to say, "It's not that Casper's not ready for babies. It's that he's a spoiled baby himself." I would love to say just that out loud, just to see how it lands. Unfortunately I can't just go around saying everything thought that pops into my head, no matter how true it might be. I've learned that lesson the hard way.

What a great world it would be, though, if we just said what we were thinking. Then I'd never have to eat my aunt's "frog's eye salad" again. No more green fluff, mini marshmallows and this tiny round pasta slapped into a giant bowl. No more gagging the glop down because when I was six I said something stupid like, "This isn't bad."

Anyway I can't get sidetracked on that because I'll really go off the rails arguing that anything involving marshmallows is not a salad no matter what else is in the bowl. That's a debate that has the potential to turn bloody among the women of my mother's church.

At least I'm not thinking about Jack's marriage proposal that hasn't happened. So there's something good about "frog's eye salad."

"I'm sorry. You've got your own problems. I should go find my mother." Cooper's voice breaks into my mental rambling. "We were all so surprised when Mom called and said Casper must've changed his mind because he let Cassie get pregnant."

I'm sorry...let Cassie get pregnant? Interesting way of putting it. Maybe Casper the Friendly Man-Child should have paid more attention in health class. Maybe instead of figuring out new ways to incorporate the Green Bay Packer logo into his funeral, Mr. Wilson should have had a little talk with his youngest boy about how it's a two person activity, getting in a family way. It's not one person allowing another person to just become pregnant.

And maybe the seed of an idea just popped into my head.

"Nora Hill?"

Cooper and I both startle when the nurse calls my name.

Oh, right. I have a concussion. I have to go see a doctor.

I look around the room. Still no sign of Jack.

Well, isn't this a nice little situation? I don't want to see a doctor. Jack's not here to make me see a doctor. Maybe I can just, you know, ignore the nurse and not see the doctor. Maybe I'll sit here long enough, Jack will come back and think I've seen someone already and he can take me home and I will order pizza because it's just occurred to me that brunch was a really long time ago and I'm hungry.

"Nora Hill?"

This time Cooper points to the nurse and looks at me. "I think she's talking to you."

"No, no, I've already been in the ER. See?" I point to Megacast. Technically, I am not telling a lie.

But Cooper is not fooled. "Come on, I'll wheel you over."

"You really don't want to go find your mother, do you?" I can't believe I said it out loud, but seriously, he's going to help me, a person he hasn't seen since he graduated college and left town, over going to comfort his mother who probably very sad and wishing her elder son was with her.

"No, Cooper, it's fine. My friend will take me in. I'm sure he'll be here very soon."

He gets up and starts moving me toward the double doors. "And you're right. I'm being terrible right now. I should be with Mom."

I'm glad I'm not looking at him. I know he's probably crying, and I don't need to see that.

"We all thought he'd grow up, that he'd get a hold of his temper, once he got married."

Cooper's voice is very low, as if he didn't mean for me to hear what he said. But I did hear him. Now his words are the water and sunshine that's making my dark little seed of a theory grow.

I know almost nothing about marriage, but I know it's not the big fix it for people who don't play nicely with others. The hope that Casper would change just because he got married ranks up there with people who believe the Tooth Fairy.

My Tooth Fairy experience was…well let's just say that when a six year old with face blindness wakes up and a stranger is looming over her bed…

I'm pretty sure my parents regretted buying me a baseball bat for my birthday that year. Although I should think they would have gotten me right into Little League once they knew I could hit hard enough to knock out my sister Lily's four front teeth. I mean any six year old who can connect from a prone position, who wouldn't want that kid batting clean up.

How did I get on the Tooth Fairy?

The nurse takes over wheelchair duty from Cooper. I glance over my shoulder hoping to see Jack…

Oh yeah, like I would recognize him. It's not like he still wears his football jersey, like he did in high school.

The double doors hiss open slowly. I feel like I'm about to enter another world. Like those kids who crawled through an armoire and wound up in a land of talking animals and permafrost.

I really don't want to do this alone.

"Nora, hold up!"

Relief washes over me. Oh no, I don't actually recognize the voice as Jack's, but I figure there aren't too many people in the ER who even know my name.

Jack puts his hand on my shoulder. "It's me, Jack."

I smell coffee and feel tremendous calm. Not that the two have anything to do with each other, other than Jack is delivering both. "What happened to you?"

"I didn't want to bother with the stuff in those little coffee stations. That brew didn't inspire a lot of confidence."

The nurse chuckles behind me. "Smart man."

"So I had to find the coffee shop. That took a little bit of looking." He hands me a warm paper cup. "I was worried you'd be in an exam room when I got back."

"Well you're just in time, Mr. Hill." The nurse wheels me into a fairly large room and closes the door behind her.

"No, I'm not…" Jack lets it drop. There's a smile on his face I've never seen before, a sort of…naughty little grin. He sits in a chair near the door and sips coffee, his lovely eyes twinkling over the rim of the cup.

"So what happened?" The nurse busies herself with my pulse, temperature, and blood pressure.

"I fell. It's no big deal."

"She fell and hit her head on concrete," Jack says.

148

"Did you black out?"

"No."

"Yes," Jack corrects me.

Maybe having him in here wasn't such a great idea.

"Which is it?" The nurse frowns at me.

"Fine. I blacked out. But it's really not a big deal. I do it all the time."

The nurse looks up from the notes she's entering into her electronic tablet. "You fall and hit your head all the time?"

"No, of course not. I black out all the time."

When I say it out loud, that sounds bad.

This triggers something in the nurse and suddenly I'm answering a series of rapid fire questions regarding my brain health. I don't have to see Jack's face to know he's enjoying my increasing discomfort during this inquisition. I'm not sure how to shake the nurse off the idea that I'm suffering from a serious brain injury. Everything I say gives her more reason to type endless, furious notes.

"Ma'am?" Jack finally pipes up.

The nurse startles, as if she'd forgotten he was in the room. "Yes? You have something to add?"

"I do. See, the black outs Nora here was referring to, those really aren't a big deal. That's all tied in to her prosopagnosia."

The nurse's face goes blank. "Her what?"

I can't believe the man learned the word. That's so sweet.

"Prosopagnosia," I respond. "Face blindness. I've had it since birth."

"She's had a ton of tests. Her brain is fine. Other than the concussion she probably got today. And…you know, the face blindness." Jack is still helpful. Less so than he was a moment ago, but still helpful.

The nurse nods as if this suddenly makes sense. "Well I'm going to have the doctor come in soon to see if you do have a concussion. She may want an MRI…"

She may want it. She's not going to get it. Nora Hill does not do magnetic pictures in a tube. That's non-negotiable. I shoot a very meaningful look in Jack's general direction.

"How did you break your leg?"

Lady, that should be in my medical files. "I kicked a stack of storage boxes my mother keeps in the garage. The boxes fell on me."

The nurse types a moment longer, stares at me for what feels like an hour, and then closes the screen on her tablet. "Okay then. The doctor will be shortly."

The doctor was not in shortly. The doctor came in almost an hour later. The silver lining was that she did not, in fact, want an MRI. She was a little too familiar with my records, having been the ER doctor that put me in Mega-cast. She ran a couple concussion tests on me, which I passed, thank you very much. She told Jack to make sure I took it easy for the next couple days. They both looked my cast and laughed, knowing I didn't have a choice in that department.

"Rest is what you need, Miss Hill. Take it easy, drink plenty of water, and maybe stop falling on concrete."

Oh she's hilarious.

I'm exhausted by the time Jack wheels me out of the exam room. Exhausted, but not ready to go home just yet. "We need to make one more stop," I inform Jack.

"We do?"

"We need to go up to the maternity floor. I'd like to see the baby." And yes, those words do sound weird coming out of my mouth.

Truthfully, I want to see the baby...unless it's still a mess, like they haven't wiped everyone down and fixed Cassie's hair and make-up. That's how they do it in the movies. Newly born babies are shiny clean and the mothers look like they just came from a day at the spa. I know for a

151

fact that's not real life, but I've had enough real life for one day. So maybe if we get up there and everything's still gross, I'll just go home and have my mother call her mother.

Because I'm nine years old and that's how I handle things.

After a couple wrong turns and a little backtracking, Jack and I manage to find our way to the maternity floor. The bright shininess of the place is a wild contrast to the stark, institutional décor of the ER. This is one of those places where labor and delivery all happen in one room. I know this because Rose insisted I join her when they toured this place right before her youngest was born. Why she did that, I haven't a clue. Like maybe she thought I'd want to be in the room for the birth? That would have been…what's the word for something that's way more than just awkward? Whatever the word is, that what watching my sister deliver a baby would have been for me.

Having now experienced the miracle of life, I'm perfectly happy to let everyone else deal with the mess and the goo and the screaming.

Anyway, Jack uses his nonthreatening manners to find out that Cassie, her mother and the newborn are, indeed, in room 417. There's a buzz in my head which I attribute to my concussion and extended exposure to overhead lighting.

Honestly, how do people work under these lights?

The door to room 417 is halfway open. As we approach the doorway, I feel a tug, a need to stop and wait. Wait for what, I haven't a clue, but I've learned to listen to any and all little messages I might get. I hold up a hand, indicating to Jack that we should wait a bit.

Inside, it's a touching scene. One woman, I'm guessing Cassie, sits on the bed, propped up by a couple pillows and draped with a blanket. An IV bag hangs overhead, probably replenishing some of the fluids she lost in the parking lot. There's a red, swollen ring around her left eye, which no doubt will be black by tomorrow. She's in a hospital gown, and even from where I'm sitting I can see bruises and scrapes on her arms. On the far side of the room, between the bed and the window, is an older woman, probably Janet. Janet is cuddling a roll of towels, which I suppose would be the baby. Jack inches my chair closer to the door, but I sense he's not eager to break up the earnest conversation they're having.

The older woman is speaking. "Darling, this was a random act of violence. The two of you were attacked and unfortunately, sadly, your beloved husband was murdered. But you and your baby survived, and you're both going to be fine." She pats the younger woman's arm, smiles, and coos at the roll of towels.

Well, older lady who's probably Janet Keen, thank you for summing up what we already know.

I'm so proud of my internal snarkiness, I nearly miss the last thing she says. "No one will ever question it."

It? Question it? What is it?

"I am sorry about your eye. Does it hurt?"

Cassie touches the red ring. "Not really. Don't feel bad. It had to be done. We had to make it look real."

"Did they test your hands?"

Cassie shakes her head. "Not yet. I'm sure they will."

"And they won't find a thing." Janet coos at the roll of towels again. "Everything is finally as it should be. You and this angel are safe and sound."

Jack puts his hand on my shoulder and tightens his grip.

I suddenly feel sick. I can't have anyone in that room see me. I need to get away, right now. A timeline of violence flashes through my head. Everything makes complete sense now and an unreasonable sense of fear washes over me. This is not what I do, this is not what I signed up for. The baby is fine. The baby is safe. I'm done, I'm out. "Jack…" I can barely choke out his name.

"Let's get you home." Jack seems to feel the same need for escape. He manages to wheel me away from the door without anyone in the room seeing us.

We reach the car and Jack gets me all settled. Finally in the car and away from the grip of the hospital, I have a bit more mental clarity and I reflect on the last ten minutes.

A big part of me believes I should alert the authorities. I mean, didn't Jack and I just hear Mrs. Keen admit she'd murdered her son-in-law? Abuser or not, that's not right.

Right?

Another part of me questions whether I heard what I really thought I heard or if I'm just mentally piecing things together, trying to make sense of a scene that makes no sense to me. I mean, distorted hearing and all…maybe I didn't actually hear what I thought I heard.

Then I realize, I don't care.

Let the adults do what they're going to do. I'm out.

That seems heartless, or immoral, or something, I'm sure, but here's the thing: Every time I have to find a missing child, I put so much into it, I lose part of myself. What part, I don't know. Maybe a piece of my heart, my soul, something internal, something I can't see. But I know it's there and I feel the tearing and breaking each time. And that's just from trying to fix some horror a child is experiencing.

If I allow myself to also get wrapped up in the horrors adults inflict upon themselves and each other, it will destroy me.

I told myself a long time ago that I would hear the still, small voice, I would open my eyes to the visions, and I would put everything I had, no matter how unwillingly, into finding lost kids. But I can't, I can't, I just can't do the same for adults. It's too hard and if that's what God wants from me, then He's going to be sorely disappointed because I just do not have that kind of strength.

Jack starts the engine, but doesn't put the car in gear. "Do you want to talk about anything...like maybe what we heard in there?" He keeps his eyes locked ahead, as if he knows turning those baby blues on me would influence me.

He's not wrong.

"Nope," I shake my head.

The rest of the ride back to my mother's house is silent. I don't know what Jack's thinking, or if he is. I, for one, am trying to lock the events of the day behind a door in my brain.

SUNDAY 5:00 PM

I'm not sure what I thought would happen next, once we get back to my mom's, but I'm weirdly disappointed that there's no "welcome home" banner or marching band on the front lawn. I mean, we did just locate someone in our church family and saved her and the baby from possible murder.

Okay, sure, most of that was Jack. But still. I heard the voice, I got us to the parking lot.

Wait, actually I just told Jack where to go. He got us to the parking lot.

Maybe God or whoever is behind the voice in my head should just talk directly to Jack and cut me out of the loop. That would make my life easier.

Jack helps me up the three steps to the porch. I'm not quite ready to go into the house. The air on the porch is warm, and still humid, but the first hints of evening dance delicately in the air, easing the most oppressive heat. We settle onto the wicker chairs in silence. It's not awkward, sitting here with Jack and not talking. I don't feel the need to escape. We just sit and watch the pink and blue and yellow lights of evening start to streak across the sky.

Jack's phone rings, breaking the spell. "Huh," he says. He walks down the steps to the sidewalk, far enough that I really can't make out the conversation. A minute later, he comes back and frowns. "That was my uncle."

"The one you're going to work for?"

"Yeah. He says he finally closed on the building, but it needs more work than he expected. He wants to move into the new location by Labor Day."

"That's two weeks."

Jack nods, but doesn't look in my direction. He leans against the porch railing, and stares at the street. "He needs me to help him with the repairs."

This is not making sense to me. "You're not a carpenter. You're a mechanic."

"I'm both, actually." He shrugs. "I'm a Jack of all trades."

I'd laugh, but I'm not finding this funny.

He finally turns his attention to me, and while his face is a blank canvas, I can't miss the tortured darkness in his eyes. "Nora, I have to go. School starts down there soon and I don't want Sam to be the new kid and a week behind, you know? I have to go. This is an opportunity for me to really support her."

The question he doesn't ask me hangs between us like a curtain. I know he wants me to join him, and I know Sam wants me to move down there. But, there is no way I'm going to St. Louis. Not for Sam, not for Jack, not for anyone. The banging in my head gets louder and the latches and locks on the door deep in my brain rattle. I squeeze my eyes shut. My mind is made up. I spent years locking away the trauma of the one time, the one time I didn't find the kid in time...I'm not going to retrace my steps back to the city and relive it all again.

Not even if it means turning down a chance to be married and be part of a family of my own.

Thankfully, Mom interrupts the awkwardness as she props the door open. She's carrying a tray, an actual tray, with lemonade. I always forget how big a throw-back she is to the 1950's. She offers a glass to Jack, who shuffles his feet on the gray painted boards of the porch and shakes his head.

"I'm sorry, Mrs. Hill. I'm actually headed out."

My mother, to her credit, keeps a broad smile pasted on her face even though I know she's wildly disappointed that he's not staying in town a bit longer. "Oh, Jack, can't you stay for dinner?"

"No, I'm sorry. I have to be getting back to my daughter. We're moving in a couple days."

"Moving?"

"Yes Ma'am. Moving to St. Louis."

"Well you have time to let me make you a sandwich for the road." Mom sets the tray on the table and heads back into the house.

"I don't have a choice about the sandwich, do I?" Jack sits in the chair next to me.

"Nope, You're going to need to wait a bit and embrace her ritual."

Mom's 'good-bye' ritual might seem pushy and intrusive, but it's actually pretty great. She never lets anyone leave her presence without some sort of sustenance for the road. She's a big believer in that Bible passage, "Whatever you did for the least of these brothers and sisters of Mine you did for me" passage. No one, and I mean no one, leaves Brenda Hill without food, drink, a jacket "just in case" and a Bible quote.

Just watch.

"Okay, Nora, look, can't you come with us? My uncle, he's got a big house, you wouldn't have to find a place right away. I've already got an apartment for Sam and me." He picks up a glass of lemonade and swirls it lightly. "I can't promise perfection. But it all could turn into something really good."

"Jack, I can't. I can't go to St. Louis." I shake my head, hoping to dislodge the look in his eyes from my brain. Can't do it.

"You could still travel, like you do. It's not like we'd try and trap you there."

"Jack, I'm a mess. You said it yourself in Superior." I feel a little mean saying this to him.

He blushes. "Nora, I was wrong about that, and you know I was. I…" he stops.

"You what?"

He takes a deep breath. "Nora, I love you, okay? I've loved you since high school. All those years in between, you know, I told you, I never stopped thinking about you and then all of a sudden you're in my life? It's like a gift, you know?" He shifts in his chair so he's looking right at me. "Before, when I told you how your mom didn't misunderstand anything. Well," he moves again, and it takes me a moment to absorb that he's on one knee. "Obviously the right moment isn't going to happen, so I'll just ask: Nora, will you marry me?"

There is it. The thing I thought we were talking about before, but I wasn't sure. Now it's there, out in the open.

I don't know what to do with this.

A normal woman would jump up and down and squeal, "Yes!" My sisters did that. My sisters are normal women.

I am not a normal woman.

So I sit there, staring at him.

He swallows and I guess he realizes he's going to have to say words or this weird silence is just going to be it. "I know. We haven't even…we haven't kissed. And I know you think…"

"You have no idea what I think."

"Fine. You're right. I haven't a clue what you think." He takes my hands in his. "But I do know a few things. I know Sam loves you. I know I love this world you've opened up for both of us. I know I love your free spirit and the fact that you just live on your own terms."

Well now he's just talking nonsense. I have to step in and stop him before he says something really stupid.

Oh, wait. He just asked me to marry him. So stopping him is no longer an option. Now I have to make him see how ridiculous this idea is.

"Jack, are you kidding me? My life is the opposite of what a guy like you should be looking for. I'm a mess. I'm a dumpster fire. You should be looking for someone…someone who's got it together more, like my mom." Did I just suggest my high school crush try to fall in love with my mother?

This is what I mean. I'm not normal. "Not that I mean you should actually marry my mother. But you know, someone like her. Someone normal, who makes lemonade and sandwiches."

"No. I've done normal my whole life. I'm not going to learn anything from normal, I'm not going to grow as person." He shakes his head. "Every time you and I are together, I learn something new. I learn how to be a better person."

"Oh like what have you learned from me?" Other than how to fall into awkward disasters in churches?

" You've taught me about courage, what it means to be a hero."

"Oh no," I yank my hand away from him. "You don't get to start using that word. No."

"Fine. Fine. But Nora, don't you see? We're good together."

"Not in St. Louis. I'll never be good in St. Louis." I think about it for a moment. Now might be the time to solve his problems so we can go back to what we were before he got down on a knee and attempted to make a gigantic mistake. "Look Jack, I have money, lots of it. Stay in Wisconsin and I'll set up a repair shop for you any place. I'll clear up whatever debts you have in Manitowoc if you want to stay there. That would make Sam happy, right?"

If I'd slapped him I doubt he could have looked more hurt. Clearly I've messed up again. Social cues are not my strong suit. Have I mentioned that?

"Nora, I have to support Sam. I can't just take your money and stay here. I have to be the one to provide for her."

"But you want me to come down there and help you."

He laughs, but there's no mirth or joy in the sound. He keeps his eyes fixed on me. "I came here to ask you to marry me, to be part of my family. I didn't come here to beg for money."

He's serious.

"Jack…"

"Of course it would be easy to let you take care of everything."

"So why don't you let me do it?"

He shakes his head. "Because, Nora, I can't. I want to marry you."

And I thought I went through life with faulty logic. I'm really not following what he's trying to tell me. "What have the two things got to do with each other?"

"Everything." He sighs and gets himself back into the chair. "How would it look, if you pay off all my debts, put me back in business, and then we get married?"

Is this a trick question? "It would look like two married people supporting each other."

"No, it would look like I married you for the money."

I'd be angry at that comment, but he's not wrong. I mean, he's Mr. All American Everything. I look like I just spent three days getting trampled at a punk rock concert. He's a solid dad person. I'm a woman who sleeps in her car more nights than she sleeps in an actual bed. I get it. Of course people would assume, if he married me, money would be the only reason.

Well, they'd probably also assume that any money I had must have come from a life of crime.

"But what does that matter?"

Jack looks confused. That makes sense. It's not like he's privy to the conversation I was just having with myself.

"Jack, look, what does it matter where you got the money? Married people support each other. That's how it works." Look at me…the marriage expert. Never been on a second date, but I've got marriage advice oozing out of me.

164

"I'm an idiot, I know it. I'm letting my pride get in the way here. Feel free to laugh at me once I'm in the car." He turns and walks down the steps, but he pauses once he's hit the sidewalk. "Besides...I don't even know if you love me."

His words are a punch to my gut. Here this guy laid himself out in front of me. He asked the biggest question a man can ask of a woman without having any idea what my answer could be.

And he says I taught him something about courage?

I might just be the worst person ever.

"Jack, you can't leave yet! I have sandwiches and a thermos of lemonade here for you." My mother bursts out the door, shattering the moment. She's got a brown sack in one hand and a jacket in the other. "I got one of Nora's father's old jackets just in case you hit some cooler weather on your way home."

What did I say about her?

"Thank you, Mrs. Hill. I appreciate it." Jack's voice is quiet, subdued. He isn't looking at me anymore. He's already distanced himself from me.

"Well, you know, I think it's in Galatians...'carry each other's burdens.' I'm just doing my part."

Meaningful Bible passage. Boom.

"Well thank you, Mrs. Hill." Jack takes another step toward the street, but he stops one last time and plants those beautiful blue eyes on me. "I hope you reconsider, Nora."

I can't stop myself. I have to say it. "Not St. Louis."

He shrugs and walks the last few steps to the street where he gets into his car and pulls away from the curb.

My mother sits down next to me and is silent for not nearly long enough. "Well now. If I didn't know better, I'd say he was asking for something more permanent than nanny help with his daughter."

I'd like to deny it. But lying is a sin. And also, I sort of pride myself in being brutally honest, no matter how much it might hurt. It's sort of my thing.

One of my things.

I have a few.

"And I'm also guessing, given the fact that he's left and you're still sitting here, that you didn't accept his offer?"

Can't get much past Brenda Hill.

"Yeah, well, he's moving to St. Louis and I'm not moving there. Anywhere but there." I'm resolute. I've made the decision. I'll worry about what I've managed to screw up later.

"Why not St. Louis?"

166

The doorknob on the door deep in my brain turns half a click. I close my eyes. I do not want to revisit the worst horror of my life. But I also don't want my mother, and most assuredly my sisters, to hound me about this until the end of time. So I take a deep breath.

"I can't go back to St. Louis."

Brenda gives me a quizzical look. "What do you mean, 'back?' When did you go before?"

This surprises me. I'd think she'd remember it. I mean, it was a long time ago, but it happened when Dad was alive and to hear her talk, that woman has never forgotten a moment of time or a single syllable of speech my father lived or breathed. "You, before. When Dad was alive. We lived there."

She shakes her head. "Nora. We never lived in St. Louis."

It might be a good thing I'm sitting down, not that I'm able stand at the moment, but I think if I were standing I would be falling. "What do you mean by that?"

"I mean, we never lived in St. Louis. We've never been to St. Louis. Now, if you have driven down there on one of your little travels..." she can't help it. Her face just twists into that disapproving grimace.

This is a shocking little revelation that she's never lived in St. Louis, my father never has, and since I know quite well that I haven't been to St. Louis since we lived there when I was a young teen...

167

Or didn't…

There's a weird, fuzzy sound, that scrambled AM radio sound, in my head again. I close my eyes. I do not want to talk about this anymore. I'm done. I want to go lie down and not wake up until everyone is done talking about the one city where I lost one child.

But, judging by the look my mother is wearing, that's not going to happen.

"Maybe it's time to tell her the truth."

I blink away the static in my head and stare at her. The words she's saying are in a tone I've never heard from her. She's not looking at me either. She's staring off into space. I could be a thousand miles away. The color has drained out of her face and her brows are knit together in a single line of concentration.

A chill runs through me. For the first time in my life, Brenda Hill is wrestling with God.

SUNDAY 8:30 PM

Apparently wrestling with the Almighty works up an appetite. Mom gets up from the chair and goes into the house. She doesn't continue her conversation with me, or with God, until she's made dinner. She sets the table full of many of my favorite dishes. And my sisters' favorites and father's and she probably whipped up a couple dishes the grandkids like.

Seriously, by the time she calls me to the dining room, the whole house smells like every holiday. I am sure the table is at least two inches shorter, having sunk into the floor with the weight of all the food.

"Um, Mom. Are you expecting someone for dinner? Like, I don't know, maybe everyone from church?"

She sits in her customary chair and she is blushing. My mother, the unflappable Brenda Hill, is blushing. It's a good look for her. She looks younger, almost girlish. "No, I just…well I cook when I'm stressed out or I'm trying to figure something out. Cooking relaxes me, helps me focus."

"Wow. What were you trying to figure out? World hunger?" I know…too obvious to be really clever.

She shakes her head. "First we say grace. Then I have some things to tell you."

I bow my head as she rattles off the table prayer I've heard since I knew what hearing was. There is comfort, steadiness, foundation in customs like this. I sort of wish the grace went on a bit. I'm not sure I'm ready for whatever it is she's going to reveal to me.

"So we never lived in St. Louis." She slaps a ladle of mashed potatoes onto my plate. "And it doesn't sound like you have been there, either."

"Except you're wrong. I have been." I rub my temples, trying to stop the throbbing in the deep corner of my mind. "I was there. It didn't turn out…well."

"Then you've been there in the last ten years?" Mom lays a thick slice of honey ham on top of the turkey leg on my plate and covers everything with gravy. Then she starts filling another plate with food.

"No. Ma, really stop." I put a hand on her arm, trying to stop her from feeding people that are not in the room. "What is going on with you?"

She turns off the electric knife and sits down. Wiping her hands on her apron, she takes a deep breath. "Okay, there's something you should know."

"I'm ready."

I'm not ready.

"When you asked earlier this summer what I meant when I said something about 'finding you' I didn't exactly answer the question."

I tap Megacast. "I'm aware of that."

She gives me a weak smile. "Here's the thing; you aren't…ours. We found you when you little."

My stomach churns. I don't know where to go with this information. So, let's try Biblical humor. "What like Moses?"

Her smile warms. "Not exactly. You were a bit older, and you weren't in a basket."

Okay, so she's not joking with me. "Was I a dumpster baby?"

"No. You were…you were just lost. We found you in Grant Park, in Chicago."

Chicago. Okay. Chicago.

"We were there on the third of July. There was a big symphony concert in the park and then fireworks. And we heard this child…we heard you crying. You were standing by the big fountain, Buckingham Fountain. You couldn't have been more than three, and you were filthy and crying. Covering your ears with your hands."

I close my eyes. Nope, never ever been a fan of fireworks. Last time I heard them I apparently pitched a fit big enough that the good people of Superior, Wisconsin, wanted to commit me to the mental hospital.

"We tried for hours to locate your family in that park. We didn't find anyone. So then we took you to the emergency room because you just wouldn't stop screaming. We explained to them what happened, how we found you."

My head is swirling. What my mother is saying somehow makes sense. I mean, I've never felt like I fully belonged in this family. But there's something else. I feel a darkness over the table. Something is about to get really ugly. I can't put my finger on it.

My phone buzzes. Oh right. It's still in my cast. I try reaching down there, but the phone just slips a little closer to my ankle. At this rate, it might be best to just wait until it hits my foot, hope it can make the ninety degree angle to my toes and just slides out that way. My mother gets up and leaves the room. Given the conversation we were having, I find the move a little heartless. However, a moment later she returns with the long handled kitchen tongs. When I was little, my sisters called them 'wiener getters.' They'd boil hot dogs and my job was to fish through the jumbled drawer of kitchen tools and find the tongs.

While I'm taking this little trip down memory lane, my mom is sliding tongs down the inside of the cast. I shiver a little at the feel of the cold stainless steel, but it's rather nice. Everything itches down there so any sensation that's not itchy is a relief. Mom knows her way around tongs. Using a move born from serving food to thousands of church people under all sorts of circumstances she manages to pull my phone out of Megacast. It's a little sweaty, but no less worse for wear.

I check the display. Sam called. And then she sent a picture. Normally I would open it and see what she has to say because the kid has a great sense of humor and chances are if she sent me a picture it's because she found something hilarious.

While yes, I could do with a good laugh right now, but I'm in no mood. I set my phone on the table, ignoring the call. Right now my attention is on my mother's immense feast and my giant cast and finding out just now that I'm adopted.

Except she hasn't used that word, has she?

Huh. Well. I should probably just ask a few questions.

"So, Mom…what are you telling me here?"

"Don't you think you should answer that message?"

"Oh no, you are not getting out of it this time. So you and Dad did what? You adopted me?"

"Well, yes. It took a long while. We actually had to live apart for almost a year. Your father's work was at a church in Milwaukee at the time. So I lived in Chicago with some friends while we waited for all the searches and the approvals and the paperwork to come through."

"Where were Lily and Rose?"

Mom clears her throat and looks a little uncomfortable. "There wasn't room at the friend's house for two girls, not for that length of time. And you know how your father was always so busy, he couldn't have taken care of them on his own. So we sent them to Grandma's."

I don't bother trying to picture Grandma Eleanor. We all know that's pointless. But I do remember her house. It was old, and creaky, and smelled like beef soup, and not in a good way.

So the whole family was split up for a year. And all because they found me.

I'm feeling totally overwhelmed by this. My sisters are devoted to Mom and I remember how close everyone was to Dad. And basically I made them all miss a year together.

In spite of that, I feel lighter. "Why didn't you tell me this before?"

She shrugs. "We didn't want you to think you didn't belong."

"What? Didn't feel like I don't belong? Do you have any idea how much I've felt I don't belong with you people? My whole life!" I'm screaming now, actually screaming.

Brenda stands up, and leans over me, very disciplining and mom-like. "Do you think we didn't struggle with this? Do you have any idea what it's like raising a child you know nothing about? We thought of you as a gift, a gift we were given."

"Some gift! You tried to make me be just like Lily and Rose, and you knew you couldn't! I felt like a failure, a disappointment, every single day!" I grab my crutches and pull myself up to a stand. I need to be eye to eye with her. She needs to understand me for once.

"You felt like a failure? How do you think we felt? You have rejected everything we believe in, everything good that we were able to give you, you turned your back on!"

"What did I reject?"

"Belonging to a church! Working in the church! Having faith! Everything your father and I hold dear, you walked away from it. And now you're here with your tattoos and your piercings and your anchorless life! Do you think I don't feel like a failure?"

So this is about her, then? Her perception of me. "I haven't turned my back on anything! I have faith in God. I just don't have faith in humanity."

"It looks the same, when you don't associate with your family, when you don't go to church." She's vibrating with a pent-up monster that is screaming to come out.

"Why on earth didn't you tell me any of this when I was younger? Do you have any idea what kind of relief I might have felt if I'd known I wasn't some lame, broken branch on the family tree, but a whole different plant? What is wrong with you? Why didn't you tell me?"

"BECAUSE!" She slams her fist on the table. The silverware jumps and jangles as it hits the hard surface. "If we told you, we were afraid you would leave us!"

This is a bucket of cold water on my head. All the spice has gone out of my anger sauce and I sit there, without an ounce of fight left. I look at her, this woman who found me and took me in, and lived apart from her family for a year just so she could adopt me.

"You were always either so scared or angry, we thought…" she sits down and takes a deep breath. "I thought you'd leave us if we told you there might be another family out there. Your father…" she wipes a tear from her eye. "Your father wanted to tell you the truth. He was always so honest. But I was afraid. I was terrified that if you left us, then you'd leave God too, and I couldn't bear the thought of feeling like we'd just sent you away from salvation."

"Mom…" I put a hand on hers. I ignore the tears rolling down my face, I try to pretend they aren't there. "I have faith, you don't have to worry about that. I'm fine that way."

"I just…I just never know if we did the right thing by you!" Mom wipes her eyes and attempts a smile.

I don't have an answer for that. Who knows if I'd turned out differently if I knew the truth? I'd still be face blind. I'd still be grumpy with God the Father for giving me face blindness. It's not a question I can answer. As good old beef-soup-smelling granny Eleanor used to say, "What is, is."

This is the first real, honest, full-blown conversation Mom and I have had, I think ever. It's a huge moment. I need to say something really affirming to make her feel better because honestly if she feels the way she looks, wow, we've done some damage here. "Mom, I don't know. I know I'm way better off with you and Dad than I would have been standing by some fountain."

She smiles and nods and pats my hand. "Thank you, Honey."

Nailed it.

We are both wrung out and exhausted beyond words. I need a bed and darkness. Brenda Hill senses this, and helps me, her youngest daughter, her found daughter, to bed in the makeshift bedroom. She pauses at the door for one moment, as if she's going to say something, but then she doesn't. She turns out the light and closes the door behind her.

In my last faintly conscious moments of this whole messed up day, I remember I left my phone on the table and I haven't returned Sam's call.

THURSDAY 11:00 AM

The funny thing about uncovering family secrets: it's made me feel closer to my family than I ever have. I'm not saying Lily and Rose and I are ever going to head up some big church committee, but in the days since my blowout with Mom, they've come around and we've talked. I feel like it's the first time they've been honest with me. Before they treated me like some sort of fragile, yet ugly, vase, something impossible to love, yet in need of constant, delicate handling. Now they speak to me as if we are equals.

Today I'm at Casper Wilson's funeral. The police released his body yesterday and Casper's family wasted no time making arrangements.

By 'family' I mean Cooper and Mrs. Wilson. The word at church is that Mrs. Wilson didn't want Cassie "troubled" with any of the funeral arrangements. The word around my mother's dinner table is that Mrs. Wilson didn't want to give up her son's remains to his wife.

Everyone's there now, though. Mom points them all out to me. Cassie, her parents, and baby Jack in the front row along with Cooper, his wife and kids, and Mrs. Wilson.

Everyone's sitting on the folding chairs, everyone's wearing the appropriate amount of black clothing and everyone's looking sad. Well, except for baby Jack who is sleeping.

Apparently, Cassie was so grateful to us that she named the baby after Jack. I bet she's thankful it was a boy. Who wants to saddle an innocent baby with a name like "Eleanor?"

I haven't told Jack he has a namesake. I haven't called or texted him. Sam's sent me countless messages, all of which I've ignored. They are, I'm sure, settled in St. Louis now, and even though I know now that I've never been to St. Louis, I still haven't sorted out what my real fear is about that city, so I'm not hopping a bus to go there. Besides, since I didn't give Jack a positive response to his marriage proposal, what's the point in continuing the friendship?

That sort of thing only works on TV, and even then, it doesn't work.

I've got my family. I've got my work. I've got an appointment with an orthopedic surgeon next week to see how much longer I have to be in Megacast. That's all I'm going to deal with right now.

It's sunny, but not as hot today as it's been. For this I am thankful. Mom is great in many ways, but providing support for me on uneven ground is not one of them. I'm forced to use my crutches, so cooler weather is appreciated. At least when I get myself to the grave site, I'm not soaked with sweat.

The service at the church was nice, I guess. It's not like I was paying attention. I was staring at Cassie and her mother, wondering about the conversation they were having at the hospital. Now, at the cemetery, I watch Janet and wonder what kind of car she drives.

I shake my head. How I can believe Mrs. Janet Keen could be capable of any kind of violence? I'm an idiot. Casper was shot by a random person. That's what the police report says. That's what everyone says.

Everyone's gathered around the casket. Cooper stands and says a few words, things like, "Casper was more than a brother, he was a friend." I'm not paying attention. I'm still staring at Janet Keen's purse. I can't help wondering if a handgun would fit in there.

Seriously, what is wrong with me?

Now our pastor, the young one my mother doesn't care for, stands up and talks about how Casper was a good church member, someone who was always there to help.

"Good church member, but not a good man."

These unexpected words come from my mother's mouth. I nearly give myself whiplash turning to look at her. Her face is placid and still, as if she hadn't spoken at all. But there's a light in her eyes I know. It's the fire that burns in her whenever she gets wind of any sort of hypocrisy.

What does my mother know?

Could she and I possibly agree on something? Does she believe that Cassie's injuries were the result of a domestic altercation, and not from the random stranger?

"They never said anything, though. You have to admire that." Again, Brenda Hill speaks, but not necessarily to me.

I follow her gaze, which is locked in on Cassie and her mother. Cassie's sitting in a chair, holding baby Jack, her mother next to her. They both sit straight, they don't move. At the end of the committal service they turn to leave the grave.

I notice neither one of them is holding a tissue. Neither of them is dabbing her eyes.

The service ends, the casket is lowered into the hole, and it's time to leave. My mother helps me back to the car. As Mom puts my crutches in the back seat I lean, for a moment, against the car. I watch as the two women I know as Cassie Wilson and Janet Keen walk down the hill to the road and get into a dark red sedan.

Instinctively I raise a hand to point at the car. I feel my mouth open, but no words come out. Mom sees my expression and steps between me and my line of sight. "It's time to go, Eleanor," she says in a low tone as she opens the passenger door. I thump into the seat and she helps me lift Megacast into place.

"There. That's done," she says.

I know she's not talking about putting me in the car. I believe she's telling me to stop thinking about Casper Wilson. This time, she's the one closing a door that should never again be opened.

FRIDAY, 9:00 AM

In my dream it's a jackhammer that wakes me but when I open my eyes, I see it's Kevin, pounding on the window just above my head. I can't believe my mom let me sleep this long. Generally she frowns upon any sleeping past sunrise. Mom likes to spout off things like, "The morning is the best part of the day," or "The early bird gets the worm," and other nonsense morning people say to annoy those of us who prefer sleeping in.

Kevin's not giving up. Kid really wants to drive today I guess.

"Just a minute!" I yell, although there's no point. I mean, lacy curtains and the pane of glass between us aren't exactly soundproof.

"Grandma's at her friends' house. She said to come over and wake you up, but I forgot until now."

Well that explains it.

Mom's at her Friday morning pre-church nitpick party. She calls it her quilting bee, but I've been there I've heard those woman jabber about everything church related. Sometimes I even feel sorry for the pastors.

181

But she can't have me sleeping the day away, so she sent Kevin over? Wow. Everyone else she knows must be busy.

"Just a minute Kevin, Let me get to the door."

I know it's going to be more than a minute. Pretty much anyone who's seen me in the last six weeks knows that making my way the nine feet from my bed to the door is going to take some time.

Except Kevin. My nephew, it seems, is impatient to get in the car and get going. Could be he's nervous. His driving test is coming up in another week and he'd like to get his license before school starts. That would be the cool thing to do. Could be he just wants to spend time with his cool Aunt Nora.

I know. It's the driving test.

By the time I get to the door, the boy is all but frothy. "What took you so long, Aunt Nora?"

I point to Megacast. "It's not like I can sprint."

"Well Mom says we have to have a fast lesson today."

"You know she doesn't mean we have to drive fast, right?"

Kevin frowns. "Yeah, I know. But she says we have to have a fast lesson today because she got the camp site at

Lapham Peak for the next three days and we are going camping there.

Lapham Peak is a state park just west of Waukesha. There is exactly one campsite. It has no electrical hookup, and no running water. And it's not near a beach. It's as close to pioneer type roughing it as my sister can find on short notice. "What did you kids do wrong?" It has to be big if Rose is taking them to the middle of almost nowhere for three days.

"I didn't do anything. The other day the twins were playing some stupid video game and it got out of hand."

"How out of hand?" The twins are seven. Whatever they've done, I know this: It's going to be entertaining…to me.

"Tristan yanked the controller out of Trevor's hands and chucked it."

Oh right. Yes, the twins are Tristan and Trevor. I mean, what did Rose think when she named them? Of course they're going to give her trouble. They're rebelling against those names. "That's it?"

Kevin grinned. "No, Tristan chucked it at Trevor…and missed."

"What did he hit?"

"Grandpa."

I blink. I'm not sure I heard Kevin right. "What do you mean?"

"You know that silver box she has on the mantle? The one with her share of Grandpa's ashes?"

I know it well.

"Tristan hit that. It opened and the bag with the ashes popped open and went everywhere. At least, that's what Trevor says."

Somehow I feel like this isn't the end of the story.

"But they wanted to cover up what they'd done, so Trevor came up with the idea that they should dust buster the ashes up and put them back in the bag."

Still not the end. Wait for it.

"So yesterday Aunt Lily comes over and says it's almost time to clean the silver boxes, you know like Grandma does with them? So Mom gets her box and she notices the latch is a little off. So she opens it."

I can't wait. "And?"

"And the ashes were in there…along with a button and two Tic-tacs."

I can't help it. I laugh out loud, and Kevin joins me. I mean, it's the first time I don't feel stupid for keeping my share of my father in the glove box.

But Kevin isn't finished yet.

"So then last night Mom's telling Dad what happened and then I remember this thing I read on Face Book. You know the Waukesha Blotter?"

I do. The Blotter is the actual portion of the police calls that are printed in the local newspaper. The writers at the Waukesha Freeman have a solid sense of humor so only the most entertaining bits from the police calls make it to the blotter. This isn't a rundown of murders or car thefts or drug busts. It's more a record of local lunacy.

"Well last week there was this thing about a woman finding an urn at a bus stop. Just an urn. No name, nothing. The lady called the cops and then the cops were trying to find who owned the urn and the ashes."

I shift my weight a bit on my crutches. I'd sit down, but I don't want to break the magical story Kevin's telling me.

"So yesterday I was reading how they found the guy that owned the ashes. It was a homeless guy who was staying at the YMCA and the ashes were his dad's."

"And you shared this story with your parents."

Kevin nods. "And that's when mom throws her hands up and says, 'That's it!' And the next thing I know, we're packing to go camping for three days."

"You didn't tell her where I keep my bit of Grandpa, did you?"

Kevin grins. "She would never let me come over here and drive with you if I did. Something about respect or something."

"Well, okay. So let's get you driving before my sister decides she wants to get an early start on your lessons in pioneering."

My phone buzzes. I realize I've left it on the nightstand next to my bed. It's probably Sam, again, but in case it's Mom, I should probably check it. "Kevin, can you get that? If I have to turn around, it's going to be longer than you want to wait."

"Sure." He trots into the house, grabs my phone from the table and returns. "It's from Sam. Is that the cute girl you know?"

"Yes, she's my...she's Jack's daughter."

"Did you tell her about me?"

Are all teenaged boys like this? "Did she text again?"

"Couple times, looks like."

"I'll look at it when I get into the car."

Kevin helps me down the steps and into the Forester and hands me my phone. He settles into his seat, and buckles his seatbelt.

I open my screen and I see several texts from Sam. The first one I read, the one from just now, says:

Nora, I just toured my new school. I hate it. I hate our apartment. Can't you please, please, please move down here?

It doesn't surprise me that Jack didn't waste time.

I scroll backwards through the other texts she's sent me this week. The first one I ignored, the one she sent Sunday night is the picture. I may as well take a look before I delete it. It's not like I'm going to recognize anyone's faces. The picture takes a moment to load, but I read the following text:

Nora: Dad says there's no reason to wait, we're leaving for St. Louis tomorrow morning. Going to drive to Madison and then the rest of the way on Tuesday. Wish you could move with us. Look what I found at the mall? Dad's wearing half, and I'm wearing the other half. So cute!

The picture finally opens. It's a picture of Jack and Sam, I guess...unless she sent me a pic of two complete strangers. They're each wearing a half of one of those necklaces where the pendants are two halves of a heart. One half says "best" the other one "friend." They're smiling as they hold their halves up for the camera.

The door in the very back of my mind explodes open in a burst of fire and thunderous noise. I have one conscious thought before the darkness takes me.

It's not the past hiding behind that door. It's the future.

I have to get to St. Louis.

Before it's too late.

Acknowledgements:

Thank you to my wonderful, faithful critique partner and friend, Linda Schmalz, who gives me advice I stubbornly refuse to take until I realize she's right about 99.9% of the time. Linda's been with me very step of the way and I couldn't do it without her.

Thank you to my dad, Dennis Schultz, who taught me grammar and sentence structure and how "spelling counts."

A GIANT thank you to my mom, Carolyn Schultz, who is so much more than just a parent who likes to line edit her daughter's books.

Thank you to my husband, Tom, who is my rock and my support no matter what goofy wild idea I have.

Thank you to Norm Bruce and the whole gang at Martha Merrell's Books and Toys in Waukesha for being so supportive of me and all independent authors. Support your local book stores! http://www.marthamerrellsbooks.com/

Finally, my biggest inspirations for this series are my children and their friends. I've watched both my children struggle with their faith and with the world. I've seen this new generation struggle to believe the truth and beauty of the Gospel both in the rigid confines of a judgmental church and in the dark faithless world. Peter and Hannah, your struggles and your optimism inspire me every day.

A Word about the Author:

S. J. Bradley lives in Wisconsin with her husband, two children, and five rescue cats. A former parochial school teacher, she has been teaching Sunday School for more than 20 years. When not writing, she searches for the perfect cup of diner coffee and soup. She hasn't found either yet, but she's come close many times.

For more information about S.J. Bradley, upcoming events, or to schedule a personal appearance, please contact her via the following:

https://www.facebook.com/sjbbooks/

https://twitter.com/sarah_theauthor

MR 5/24

Made in the USA
Monee, IL
21 February 2024

53343707R00105